KANE 3

King Coopa J

KANE 3

Available on Amazon

Lifted: Power Money and Speed

Kane

Kane 2

Taste

Coming Soon

The Japanese Messenger

Eagle

Chapter 1: Kane

Touchdown. I dunked the football through the goal post. *Champions.* I ran to the sideline to look for my father. Everyone was celebrating, making it harder to spot him. I finally found him. He was standing in the middle of a crowd with a dissatisfied look on his face as if he wasn't happy. I stopped ten feet away from him. Something was wrong, so I took off my helmet. A more serious look replaced the smile on my face. I approached him. He didn't say anything, not one word. He looked at me in disgust. "What's wrong?"

What came out of my father's mouth shocked me. "Why is Abel still alive?"

Suddenly, I heard Kim call my name. My vision became blurry for a second before focusing on the face in front of me. She was just as beautiful as the first day I met her.

"You had a bad dream."

She looked worried. "It was the same dream as before."

"The one about your father?" She sighed.

"Yeah," we were home from the hospital. It's been a month and I had this dream five times. I didn't want her to worry about me. She'd been through enough, and I won't let anything happen to her again. I would die for her. "It's ok. You don't have to worry."

"Your father wants you to revenge his death. That's why you have bad dreams." She said, concerned. "You guys have been through a lot together. It shouldn't have to be this way. His soul won't rest until Abel is dead."

She was right about Abel tormenting my father's soul. We had plenty of father-son moments. That day on the football field, my father congratulated me before we hugged. I remember the day vividly.

I caressed the side of her face and smiled. "I know you care, but everything will be ok. I know what I have to do. Not only for my father…you as well."

I broke through to her, and she smiled. "I love you, Kane Simmons."

"I love you," we kissed passionately.

She pulled back and slapped my forehead, playfully. "Get up, and I'll make breakfast."

"Slap my forehead again if you want me to kick your butt," I joked.

She popped the center of my head. "Do something."

"Oh, you want me to do something?" I grabbed her waist and began tickling her. She started laughing uncontrollably and tried to escape my hold. "Ok, I got you." I pulled her closer to my body, working my fingers in every area that would make her cry.

"Stop, please stop." She laughed harder and tickled my side, trying to defend herself. "No mas."

"That's right," when I released my grip, she slapped my forehead and quickly sprung from the bed. "I'm gonna get you!" I shouted as she ran out of the room. I sighed. "Women."

I slowly got up from the bed and stretched my arms and legs. A ray of light shined through the window, and I walked over to open the curtains in my bedroom just enough to see the morning sun. Kim and I have been staying at my house ever since Abel been on the run. My mother had been kidnapped from the hospital, so I control the property until otherwise. There wasn't a reason to worry about my brother showing up unless he wanted to die. I haven't heard anything from him. Every now and then, Smoke or Bear would stay overnight to watch for anything suspicious. We haven't made any moves with the money. Kim was shocked after I told her we have 23 million dollars. Her eyes popped out of her head when I opened the briefcase.

I feel much better than before. My stab wound was healing just fine. I give it another week before I'm 90 percent. When I fully recover, I'll search for The Planner. That's the only way to find my mother in time. He wants to trade her for the diamond or the money. He might want both. After I handle that situation, I'll find Abel and put him in the ground so my father's soul can rest.

I looked over to my neighbor's backyard and smiled. "My fault, big dawg." The recovery cone around the neck of the dog who attacked me looked like a lamp. I felt sorry for tossing him into a wall, but he was about to kill me. Every time I looked out of the window, he was there waiting for me to show my face to remind me of what I did to him. I shook my head. "You're not the only one who wants me dead." I shut the curtain and got in the shower. After twenty minutes, I made my way downstairs into the kitchen with Kim. The aroma in the air spoke to my stomach.

Yeah, I'm hungry.

I looked over at her. She was doing her thing while dancing to the music. I stepped behind and grabbed her waist. "Callaloo and shrimp? It smells good."

"Thank you," she eased her head under my chin.

She looked up, smiled, and kissed my lips. "I'll be back. I need to check on Bear. He fell asleep in my father's office."

"He was looking for anything Abel might have left behind." She began mixing the Callaloo."

"Bear," I sighed. "I told him I searched it several times and didn't find anything. He's determined to find something. Abel can't hide forever, and the police are after him. I need to find him before then."

"Where do you think he's hiding?" She turned down the music.

4

"I don't know," I said honestly. "I have a friend from high school that's helping decode everything in Abel's laptop. Asian kid, Smoke put me in contact with him."

"Do you trust him?"

"I don't have a choice." I picked up the spatula and tasted the food. "Delicious."

"Hey." She slapped my hand.

"Ok, I'll be right back." I left the kitchen and walked to the office. The door was left open, and I pushed through. I spotted Bear sleeping in my father's chair with his head down and arms crossed on the desk. "Bear, get up," I shouted as I got closer. To my surprise, it worked.

Bear's head shot up from a resting position. "I'm up." He said frantically.

I smirked, stunned that it didn't take any effort to wake him. Usually, I had to scream in his ear or shake him. "Kim's cooking Calloloo, it'll be ready soon

." I turned back to the door."

"I had a dream."

I stopped and turned around. "Me too. I had the same one about my father this morning. Trust me, we all been through hell."

"It wasn't like that." He sounded serious.

My facial expression changed, and I got a little concerned about the worried look in his eyes. He never before shared with us any of his dreams. The look on his face said the same.

What he said next shocked me. "We were searching for Abel in Africa."

Chapter 2: Jordan

I drove the car through the woods down a long dirt road. A log cabin came into view. The place appeared deserted on the inside. All of the lights were off, and the driveway leading up to the house was empty. I visited this place every summer when I was younger. It was where my brother and I learned to survive in the wild. My father trained us, and we became skilled hunters by the age of ten and eleven. I haven't spoken to him since I became a cop. It's been years since then.

I stopped the car in front of the cabin and turned to Mrs. Simmons. It's been a month, and I thought about killing her every-single-day. She's overly beautiful, but looks are deceiving, and I'm sure she'll slit my throat the first chance she gets. I can't trust anybody, and that's how I like it. Me against the world. "This is the place."

Mrs. Simmons glanced around the property. "It doesn't look like anyone is home. If you cannot hold up your end of the deal. I suggest-"

"Then I'll kill you." I interrupted. She faced me, and I looked deep into her eyes when I spoke, so she felt the situation's seriousness. "Remember, you need me. I'm still debating if I should trust you. Wait here, and don't get out of the car. I don't want to put a bullet in your head just yet." I held eye contact with her for a few seconds. She didn't break a sweat at any point in our stare down. I smirked and got out of the car.

Don't let your pride get you killed, Mrs. Simmons.

I sighed and scanned across the front of the cabin. "Where the fuck are you?" I muttered. Not only can my brother fly a plane, but he is also a master hunter. Just not the kind that hunts animals. That's why we grew apart when I decided to pursue law enforcement. He became a hitman for hire. Flying is a part of the job. At one point in my life, I wanted to bring down bad guys like him. But that all changed when I went undercover in the Mob. Those were the best days of my life.

My eyes ran up the pathway to the first step. When dealing with a man who kills for a living, you have to be mindful of booby traps. I cautiously began walking toward the front door, continuing to scan the area as I approached. "Adrian," I called out his name with my hands high to display I wasn't a threat. "Adrian, it's me. Your brother." I tried to peek through the left side window. He had smeared dirt on it. I couldn't see anything on the inside. "Fuck." He's the type of guy who knew you were at the front door. I don't know of anyone who can show up by surprise, and he wasn't aware of their presence.

I heard a voice in the distance. "Try the back."

I swiftly turned around and spotted Mrs. Simmons standing by the car. "Don't hurt her!" I yelled. Adrian stood behind Mrs.

Simmons, ready to attack. I should have known something like this would happen if I brought her along.

I'm a fucking idiot.

"Ah!" She yelped as my brother grabbed her from behind and put a blade to her throat.

"Adrian." I held out my hand, trying to ease any uncertainty about us being here. A surge of anxiety stormed through my blood cells. My mind said, draw your weapon and have some fun.

Cat and mouse sound about right.

No. Shut the fuck up, Planner! I can't get dirty right now.

I have to keep Mrs. Simmons alive if I want the money. *Damn, I hate saving people.*

Lately, I have been thinking as The Planner and agent Jordan. It's as if I'm indecisive about who I want to be. "She has a deal for you, and trust me. You need to hear what she has to say." That wasn't part of the plan, but what the hell. If he kills her, she brought it upon herself.

Mrs. Simmons squirmed in my brother's arms before relaxing in his grip. There is nothing she could do to escape. My brother had control of her life. Lucky for her, she wasn't dead yet. Where was the woman I saw in the office? The crying bitch, looking for attention because someone murdered her weapon smuggling husband.

9

She's changing by the second.

I'm learning more about her fearless persona as time pass. *Keep revealing to me who you really are, Mrs. Simmons.*

Adrian stood there without moving an inch. His eyes appeared to be black, somewhat vacant. Abel reminded me of my brother. Two lives filled with anger and death. The blade remained pressed against the neck of Mrs. Simmons, sharp enough to cut her head off. Regardless of its size, weapons used by the man in front of me are for fatal blows. Fatality is the only outcome when in war.

"I'm not here to arrest you." I stepped off the porch with my hands down by my side. *Fuck it.* My hands needed to be by my gun. If she dies, she dies. I still have to kill Kane, if anything, for embarrassing me in front of the world. Adrian is deadly, and I had to be ready if he tried to make a move. Deep down, I wanted him to get active. "The woman you're holding can pay you more than double your fee." I stopped approaching midway to keep a safe distance, letting what I said to settle in his mind. "We need you to fly us to Africa. Her dead husband built a smuggling business. He stashed millions of dollars in a safe house, and she's the only person who knows the passcode. That's why I need her. I went out of my way to kidnap her from a mental hospital. Of course, you know I've gone rogue. I made a deal with the Africans, and they think I betrayed them. I wouldn't go there to die. She wants to hire you to fly us there, and if the situation gets dirty, well, you know the deal. This is not a one-man job. After I get my cut, you can fuck off."

Suddenly, Mrs. Simmons fell out of his grip and then turned around to face him. "He's telling the truth. I'm the only person who knows the location of the safe. My husband didn't trust anyone to help. He built the safe house with his bare hands. I stood by his side every day until the task was complete. If it's not there, the remainder of my life depends on you."

My brother made eye contact with me, then put his attention back on her. "The price is triple, three million."

Chapter 3: Abel

I walked out onto the back deck of our family beach house. Jar purchased this as a type of staycation for us five years ago. It's a shame we only came once as a family. That's what you call a father. Spend your hard-earned money where it counts. Kane is a knucklehead. He wouldn't look for me here, although I should not underestimate his intelligence. He found out I murdered our father.

Brother vs. brother, I accept the challenge.

My focus had to remain on getting the diamond to Africa. That's why I'm here with the rest of my crew. Kane could wait to die at a later date.

There is a pilot who goes by the name Silva. His name popped up several times in the black notebook. He used to fly for Jar and made a fortune working for him. The beach house across from ours belongs to him. Who would have thought they were that close? In a matter of seconds, I found all of his information on the internet. I decided to lay low for a while until the heat died down. Only then would it be safe to fly. As of yet, I didn't come across any headlines regarding my name. I used a secure line to hack into the FBI criminal database to clear any warrants for my arrest. What is the use of being a genius if you can't use your intelligence to create an advantage?

"Good morning," I heard a lovely voice from behind.

I sensed Gina by my side. She leaned on the balcony next to me, close enough to touch. "Good morning to you, beautiful." I meant it. She is not like any other woman I've ever met. Her heart is just as cold as mine, and she's dangerously deceptive to anyone lower than her intellectual level.

"You need to speak with Sliva today," Gina spoke in a soft tone.

"He hasn't returned since last night." I didn't look at her when I spoke. The morning sun shined across the water, highlighting the breathtaking scenery. The kind of view that could win any woman's heart.

"You need to rest." She said. "I'll take over and if he shows himself. I'll wake you, my love." She leaned her head against my shoulder.

"Don't worry about me." A year ago, I only thought about taking over the government and becoming the underworld's unquestioned alpha boss. Gina slightly altered my perspective of women. She implements the things Jar used to teach me to be aware of when it came to women. I'm aware of the effects she has on my decision-making. I feel like I have to protect her. I wondered if this was how Kane felt about Kim when he first met her? If so, Gina could stand in the way of a life-time awaited victory.

"I won't press the issue." She said. "I think we need to get rid of Bam."

The news wasn't shocking. I already knew how she felt about Bam, and I began to feel the same energy. After he left Snake for dead in the hands of an enormous freak of a man, Bam wouldn't survive in Africa. The rebels would tear him apart. I'm intelligent enough to realize she tried to provoke me to perceive that he's weak. "We can't afford to lose a brain that operates as we do. Manpower is crucial at this stage. Cutting him off now won't accelerate anything forthcoming. You need to be patient. His time will come. I promise."

She sighed. "It's Silva. His boat is pulling up to the dock."

My eyes followed in the direction of Gina's finger. An exotic blue and yellow four-passenger speed boat docked fifty yards away. A skinny, dark-skinned man hopped off the boat with a woman wearing a two-piece bikini. They embraced, and it ended with a kiss before they entered the beach house. The windows were open, and I could see through into the bedroom. I guess he didn't care if anyone was watching, and I've waited all night. I hope he's ready to fly.

Chapter 4: Rick

"Lower your fucking gun!" I yelled while aiming my pistol at a former informant who worked for Jordan, or should I say, The Planner. Whoever the hell he is, this sonofvabitch worked with Jordan when he was undercover. Jordan told me everything about Frankie, and I finally tracked him down in an Italian restaurant on the southside of town. If anyone had information on Jordan, it's Frankie the Snitch. The guy who brought down TMF single-handedly by running his mouth. "Frankie, tell your guy to put down his weapon. I just want to talk." Five kilos of what I assume to be heroin sat on the table in front of him.

Frankie's eyes went from the packages to the barrel of my gun. "I can't do that."

I scanned the room to make sure no other thugs were in proximity. We were in the back of the restaurant in a room where all of the deals went down. I had cased the place for a month, watching Frankie's every move. A small-time dealer gave up information that led me here. I let the guy go after I got the details I needed to find the place. The streets would deal with him. These days nothing goes unheard. "This can go easy, or it can get really fucking bad. It's up to you, Frankie. I'm not here for the dope, but I can be if that's how you want this to go down."

Frankie smirked. "Trust a fucking copper?" He spat on the ground in disgust.

I hate to think about it, but I remembered how Jordan used to handle wise guys like Frankie. The one thing you look for when talking to a mob guy is respect. If you want respect, you have to earn it or take it by force. This situation was no different. I knew what I had to do. The guy with the gun aimed at my head looked like he'd done this before. He wouldn't hesitate to pull the trigger. There is one thing I'm good at, and that's hitting my target.

BOOM!

"Ah!" The gun flew out of the goon's hand and hit the ground.

"Don't move." I swiftly shifted my weapon on Frankie's head.

"You stupid cock sucker." Frankie snarled. His hands gripped the edge of the table after attempting to make a sudden escape.

"I could have killed him." Frankie's guy was on the ground crying about his hand. Blood covered his arm sleeve and the bottom of his shirt. *He'll live.* I made my point without having to commit murder. He had a gun on me, self-defense if anything. "You have a shit load of dope in front of you."

"I'm not going back to the Big House." He growled. "You'll have to kill me first."

"What about your wife and kids," I asked.

"Are you fuckin' threatening my family?" Frankie stood from the table fearless and pointed at his chest as he spoke. "Are-you-fuckin' threatening my family-you fucking-pig?"

"No," I assured him. "The Mob already suspects you to be a snitch. I see five kilos of dope sitting on the table. That's a life sentence for a guy like you. If I take you in, and let's say around five in the afternoon, you're let go. What would your friends think of you?"

Frankie studied my face for a moment before speaking. "What do you want?"

"Jordan," I told him without hesitation. "Tell me where I can find him?"

"I don't have the slightest idea where to find that fuckin' rat." Frankie pounded his fist on the table. "He's the reason why I'm in this situation in the first place. I got the blame for working with a fuckin' undercover cop. I didn't bring the rat into the house. If I knew where to find him, I'd put a bullet in his head."

"Do you know of Black Water?" I asked. Frankie seemed more placatory as we spoke.

"I'm gonna fuckin' kill you!" The goon yelled from the floor.

"Shut the fuck up, Tony." Frankie turned to his guy when he spoke. "You fuckin' idiot. I'm talking business over here." His attention came back to me. "Everyone in the Mob knows about

17

Black Water. The hitman that never misses. The guy is a stone-cold killer. What business do you have with a monster like that?"

"I know Black Water is Jordan's brother," I told him. I found out, Adrian, Jordan's brother, is a hitman for hire. Over fifty jobs for the Mob, and that doesn't include the work he has done in other counties. Who knows the exact body count. After Jordan revealed himself as a crooked FBI agent, it's automatic to complete an extensive background check on his entire family. That's when I found deleted files in the system involving Adrian. Jordan was covering for his brother the whole time. Nobody had a clue, not even me. "If I can find him. I got Jordan."

"If I tell you where you can find Black Water," Frankie's attention went on the packages. "I keep the blow, and you never fuckin' came here, deal?"

I caught eye contact with him and lowered my weapon. "Deal, where can I find him?"

"Nobody knows about this but me, so if it gets out. I know it was you." Frankie gave me a skeptical facial expression. "Jordan told me about a cabin his father used to bring them to in the summer for training, mostly hunting their prey. If what he said is true, Black Water could be there using the place as a hideout until he gets a job. It's the perfect place for a guy who's trying to avoid the meat wagon."

"The location of the cabin?" I asked.

18

"It's in the backwoods further down south." He said. "The place is surrounded by woods. You should consider your options. If you're not going there to offer a deal on someone's life, watch your own. If you're lucky, Black Water won't be there to kill you."

I thought about the proverbial circumstances. Jordan is a mastermind, killer, and a fucking great cop. He taught me everything I know about the streets, even trust. This could mean my life. If Jordan is hiding out with his brother, that's a new level of danger, an expert FBI agent who knows how we operate in cahoots with a professional hitman, and they trained together when they were younger. I asked myself, *am I ready to deal with that?* "Location?"

Chapter 5: Kim

"Hey," I slapped Kane's hand to keep him from eating any more of the Callaloo. It was just about ready. He could wait.

He pulled his hand back and put down the spoon. "Ok, I'll be right back."

After he left the kitchen, I continued cooking the food. I turned the music up a bit and swayed to the beat.

I woke up every morning and cooked breakfast. It's been a week, and I felt stronger each day that went by. Kane had been by my side every step of the way. He never counted me out when I slipped into a coma for over a month. I felt him while I slept. My love for him had grown even more despite what Abel did to me.

I will get revenge.

I grabbed three plates from the top left cabinet. I became familiar with the kitchen over the summer, Kane's sophomore year. Mrs. Simmons asked for my help on several occasions when preparing a large meal for the family. That's when Kane and I decided to take our relationship seriously. "Bear," I added more food on his plate and placed it on the table. "Kane," I muttered, making his plate. The last dish was for me. "The food is ready!" I shouted after turning down the music.

Suddenly, I began to feel light-headed. I haven't felt like this since the first day I left the hospital. My right hand could barely hold the plate of food. My version became blurry, and I got scared. "Ah!" I cried out as I fell to the floor. The sound of the plate shattering echoed in my ears. I managed to prop my back against the bottom cabinet under the sink.

"Kim!" Kane's voice sounded hysterical as I watched him rush into the kitchen.

He ran over and dropped to a knee beside me and gently held the back of my head. The fear I felt when I was blindfolded and tied down momentarily emerged in my mind. A glimpse of Abel taking advantage of my body flashed before my eyes, and I instantly became terrified reliving that experience.

"Is she ok?" I heard a touch of concern in Bear's voice.

"Kim," Kane had an emotional tone when he said my name. "is everything ok? What happened to you? Are you hurt?" He checked for any harm done to my body.

"I'm... ok," I told him. "I tripped and fell." I thought about telling Kane the truth about what happened and decided against it. He didn't need to worry about anything other than his mother. I'd deal with what I saw. This could be temporary, and another concern would be overwhelming on his mental. I didn't want him to think of it as a complication or a side effect due to the coma. For now, I kept the problem to myself.

"You fell?" Kane asked skeptically.

They looked around on the floor.

Hopefully, I convinced them. I tried to move, but my legs and butt ached. The fall could have been severe enough to cause a head injury. I got lucky.

"Lemme help you."

Kane lifted me off the floor with ease. He was substantially stronger than before he went to jail. It's incredible how his body transformed over the years.

"I'll clean up the mess," Bear said.

"Thank you." I looked at Bear while Kane carried me over to the table, slid a chair out with his foot, and placed me in it.

"No problem, sis." Bear grabbed a broom and began cleaning. "You're the one who cooked the food."

"How does your head feel?" Kane asked worriedly.

"This is what I don't want you to do," I said seriously. It was the only way to get him to understand while not getting his feelings hurt.

Kane reserved a special place in his heart for me. He's a compassionate and kind-hearted person. Understanding something like this would not be easy, especially when feelings were involved. I needed him focused on what was ahead.

Abel will get what's coming to him for murdering their father and for what he did to me.

"What are you talking about?" He asked with a raised eyebrow.

"I know how much you love me, but I don't want you to worry," I said as the expression on his face changed from concerned to shocked. "You have other things to do that are more important. I saw the look in your eyes when you came over to help. I'm a big girl. I just fell, that's it."

"It's just," He started and then looked down as if he was hurt by what I said. "When I thought I lost you, I felt a piece of my soul tear away from my heart. Now that I have you back, I'll never let that happen again. No matter the cost. I will protect you. I don't care if it's something small or big. I'll be there for you, but I do understand what you mean. You're a strong woman, and that's why I love you."

I couldn't help but smile. Kane means everything to me. I never want to think about what if he grew tired of me? That's something I didn't ever want to occur. For him to understand what I'm going through was meaningful in many different ways. If another image of Abel flashed like that in my head, I'd have to speak about it with Kane. I control my life, not Abel. I won't allow someone the authority over my mind. Crying is supposed to help free yourself emotionally if you were a victim, then face reinsuring yourself. And motivate your inner self to become the person you were before the incident. That was not how I felt or desired to transpire in my situation. The day Abel kidnapped me from the mall and forced himself on me would impact my life forever. I'd overcome this by not letting Abel win.

Unexpectedly, Bear spoke up. "She's right about being a big girl. I wasn't scared at all when I saw her on the floor. I mean, she did flip over multiple times in a van. Think about it. That's some superhero shit."

Chapter 6: Kane

"Ok, you're right." I'm sure she perceived the seriousness in my eyes. "You can handle yourself. Just know I will always be there when you need me, Superwoman." I smiled to ease the tension.

I could be over protecting when it came to people I love. What Abel did to our father crushed me, and a monster kidnaped my mother. Trying to keep my emotions in check became more of a task every second of the day. I had to protect the people I care about the most. This group of ours is the only family I have left.

"Someone is at the door," Bear said as he focused his attention on the doorbell.

"It's Smoke," Kim said from the chair. "I called him this morning and told him to come over if he wants breakfast."

"Cool," Bear said, heading out of the kitchen. "I got it."

I sat at the table next to Kim. "I know you're alright, but I have to ask again."

She smiled at me. "I'll be alright under one condition."

"What is that?" I asked.

She looked at the floor where she fell. "I dropped my food, and my stomach got upset about it."

"That's it?" I asked, ready to offer help. "No problem. I'll clean up and serve you another plate." I got up from the table and heard a familiar voice."

"Make that two plates, my guy."

"Smoke," My best friend walked into the kitchen, and we dapped hands.

"I got you," I said. "Only if you clean the floor?" I pointed to the mess.

"Man…" He sighed. "I just got here."

"I don't work for free."

"Sis," Smoke turned his attention on Kim.

"If you want to eat." She replied with a shrug.

"Ok," Smoke surrendered. "y'all got me."

Smoke grabbed the cleaning supplies from the closet and went to work. Bear sat at the table across from Kim. I came back to the table with the food. "Here you go."

I served Kim a dish and sat the other plate in front of an empty chair for Smoke.

"Thank you." Kim inhaled the aroma of the food then began to eat.

"Like Bear said," I paused and took in the pleasant smell of the Callaloo. "you cooked."

Smoke finished cleaning and joined us.

"I feel like I could've made the plates, and you should've cleaned the mess." Smoke said.

Kim laughed, and so did Bear.

"I know now," Smoke looked at me. "I got the raw end of the deal."

I smiled at him. "That was an option."

Smoke sighed. "I have to stop smoking early in the morning, but I'm hungry as hell."

"Done," Bear said. "delicious."

I couldn't believe he finished eating that fast.

"I should've put more on your plate," Kim questioned.

"No worries," Bear got up from the table. "it was just enough. Excuse me."

He rinsed off the dish in the sink.

"So, what do we have planned for the day?" Smoke asked before trying the food.

"We need to visit Tang," I told him. "See if he has any new information. Then contact Rick and find out if there is any development in my mother's case."

"Good idea," Smoke said.

Bear came back to the table. "Who is Tang?"

"The goofy Asian kid who used to follow us around in high school." Smoke continued eating.

"Oh, the young dude," Bear recalled. "the genius. He's still around. I thought he would be the president by now. That kid did all of my homework just to hang with the crew."

"Nevertheless, he hasn't changed one bit." Kim finished the food and slid the plate slightly forward. "I'm stuffed."

"His father built a technology company, and Tang is in control of the business," I said. "He's on the same level as Abel, maybe even smarter."

"I'm going to lay down while you guys are gone," Kim spoke up. "I need some rest."

"Good idea," Bear said. "At least somebody is getting the proper sleep around here."

"What are you talking about, big fella?" Smoke said.

"I've been up lately," Bear said. "Ever since I began visiting a therapist, I don't sleep as much."

"The sessions are working?" Smoke asked, finishing off his food.

"I think so," Bear looked for the right words. "or, worrying about you guys has kept me up. I've never felt like this before. I think the day we pulled up on Abel changed everything. I feel more alert because of him."

"Interesting," Smoke picked up my plate and Kim's. "I got it." He took them to the sink. "A bit of extra work doesn't hurt."

Ding dong.

28

The doorbell, I thought.

"Who could that be?" Kim asked. "I wasn't expecting anyone else."

"Me, either," I said. I got up from the table and walked to the door. The person on the other side shocked me. He was bigger than I remember. My hand rested on the doorknob, debating if I should open it.

"Kane," My name rang out from the other side of the door.

He knows I'm home.

"There is no reason to be scared."

Suddenly, I heard footsteps behind me.

"Bruh, bruh," it was Smoke. "you good?"

I didn't answer, nor did I turn around to acknowledge him. My eyes stayed glued to the door. Sweat began to form on my forehead. *Damn, I'm sweating.* "Get ready."

"Wha?" Smoke sounded confused.

"It's the guy I told you about from jail," I said and turned the knob. The door opened to a massive man, slightly shorter than me but looked more powerful than an ox. He grinned, and we locked in a stare. "Big Bruce."

Chapter 7: Jordan

Adrian led the way into the cabin, followed by Mrs. Simmons and then myself. I kept Adrian in my line of slight as we entered one at a time. Assuringly, this band of three had trust issues. I didn't expect coming here would go exceptionally well. A skilled hitman, widow, and a jack of all trades all working together.

Who would have thought?

My so-called brother became a pain in my ass. Dead bodies began to pile up around Atlanta. *My city.* I was just a rookie cop at the time, fresh out of law enforcement school. I had a dream to be the best damn cop in the city. Everything changed when I discovered Adrian was the corporate who committed the crimes under a codename, Black Water.

Black Water became a household name among prominent figures with the power to get shit done. He didn't only kill for money. It was deeper than one could imagine. The victims were predetermined murders. The crime scenes became nightmares, visually haunting while I slept. The time we spent together training with our father paid off.

A senator was shot in the head the day I got promoted to special agent in the FBI. The sniper turned out to be Adrian. The hit wasn't a contract job. It was my brother's way of saying congratulations and fuck you at the same time. I didn't say a word when I received a text from a private caller that read, *you're the man.* That was something my father used to say when I performed well in the field. Adrian hated it because our father never said those words to him. I was flat-out more skilled than Adrian at the time. In retrospect, maybe Adrian took that to heart, which gave him a reason to be a hitman after I became a police officer.

Adrian flicked on the light in the living room. The place smelt of firewood as if he had been here for some time. The space was surprisingly clean, and the furniture looked new. I couldn't tell before from looking through the outside window.

Mrs. Simmons' eyes wandered around a bit before they settled on Adrian. She didn't appear to be scared of him. Her body movement and speech were limited as if she restricted from being herself. I could sense she wasn't comfortable, and maintaining a good composure had to be hard. Somehow, she did without exposing how problematic it was for her.

"You live here?" She spoke calmly.

My brother didn't answer right away. Instead, he ignited the fireplace and stood there as if he was deep in thought. At that moment, I realized how cold it was inside the cabin. I was focused on Adrian the entire time to notice a climate change after we stepped from outside. *I should kill him for all the bullshit he put me through while I was a cop.* I had to pretend Black

31

Water was another serial killer out to make a name like the others before him. *Bastard.*

"Sure," Adrian responded nonchalantly. "you can say that."

"Does the old man know you're here?" I spoke to get him to open up about why he's here. My eyes trailed up to a picture framed on the wall above the fireplace. It was a photo of the family my father hung there our first stay.

"What does it matter to you?" He said, looking up at the picture. "As far as I'm concerned, you're not a part of his legacy, what he created for us, and our grandfather before him...what they strived for us to become to honor the family name in which you deny. Jordan, who is that? I thought your last name was Campbell."

I knew it would come to this if we ever had a conversation. I changed my last name when I decided to join the police force. My grandfather worked with the Italian Mafia in Detriot. That's our family's birthplace, and we only moved to Atlanta to escape judgment. What people thought about us didn't matter to my father, and raising two boys alone proved to be a challenge. The average person knew the history of our last name. My grandfather and father had a combined body count of over six hundred, and my brother and I added to that number over the years.

"Who the fuck are you to tell me about family legacy?" I snapped. It wasn't Jordan talking anymore. The Planner took over on my behalf. "I fought hard to make a name for myself. I wanted to be somebody, not a fucking hitman for hire. Look at how we were raised and tell me there was a future for us in high society?"

"But you couldn't escape your destiny." He said and turned to face me. "Look at you now. You're a real American hero, sitting at the bottom of the pit with no one to love or care for you."

"I don't need anybody, especially not you or our shameful family name," I said sternly. "After this is over, I'll be set for life. Love is a strong and overused word. Start a family, and then your wife decides she wants a divorce. One mistake could leave you with a life full of regret. I don't see an American dad in front of me. I see a cold-blooded killer. Well done, little bro."

"Do I have to sit here all day and listen to you both go at it?" Mrs. Simmoms spoke up. "I thought we agreed to make some money? Stop bickering, and let's come up with a plan. At any rate, if we're on bad terms, we'll die in Africa. I seen with my own eyes what the army does to their enemies. We need to be on the same page before taking on such a task. If you both need to go out back and fight, do it. Get it out of the way if that's what it will take to get focused on what we're about to confront."

I looked at Mrs. Simmons. "I'm two seconds away from blowing your goddamn head off. This is not your moment. This is about that sonofvabitch over there who ruined my life. Just know I could've caught you, but I decided to spare your miserable excuse for a career. It was the least I could do for my little snot nose brother who cried when father praised me."

"And you should know that bullet wasn't meant for the senator." He said. "I had a contract on your head, but I decided to spare your miserable excuse for a career, big brother."

I couldn't respond. Black Water had come for my life, and didn't take it. Deep down, I know I should be dead if that was the case. My brother doesn't miss his targets. Once the contract is signed, you're finished. *He spared me, but why?*

After a brief staredown, he said. "The woman is right. We need to focus on a plan if we're to get through this. I've been to African once. I had accepted a contract on a public figure, causing an uproar with the government. I didn't find out it was the current president's cousin until after the job."

"So, you're not welcome there either?" Mrs. Simmons asked.

"No," Adrian replied. "I'll have to hide my identity after we land, or there will be an all-out war."

"That's fucking great," I commented before walking out of the cabin.

34

Chapter 8: Abel

I smirked because the wait was finally over. The time was now. Silva has no other option but to accept the offer I had for him.

Gina looked at me and said, "How do you want to proceed if he doesn't cooperate?"

Gina, Gina, Gina, I thought. *You have an evil little mind.*

"Violence isn't the key," I told her. "Don't forget, we need him to be in flying condition. We can't risk any bodily harm to him. There are other methods to get him to cooperate."

A grin spread across Gina's face.

"It's time," I told her.

"Ok, should I let the others know?" She asked.

"We can handle this by ourselves." I looked at the beach house one last time before leaving the balcony.

Gina followed close behind and shut the door as we left.

Silva was small in size compared to me. His skinny frame looked around one hundred and twenty pounds. I'm well over two-twenty and built like a bull. There won't be a problem, and if so, I'll let Gina have some fun.

We both left the house without alerting Snake or Bam. I didn't bother to grab a weapon. Murdering Silva was not on my mind. Surely, Gina wouldn't think twice about taking care of business if it came down to it. If things did get out of hand, I'd stop her before she went overboard.

I walked to the front door like anybody would do when visiting someone. I'd watched the place all night until he had arrived with the woman. Nobody else was inside but them. Silva or the woman didn't think to lock the door. His mind was on pussy. In his line of work, that could get you killed if you're not careful. Like at this very moment, for example.

I put my hand on the doorknob and turned as if I owned the property. Like I'd thought. The door was unlocked, and we stepped past the threshold. Gina entered first, and I quietly shut the door behind us.

Right off the bat, I could tell Silva was from our homeland. That had to be the reason Jar worked with him. He was one of us, a Jamaican. A large flag representing our country covered the living room wall. I heard reggae music combined with a powerful stench of ganja.

Somebody is having a good time.

The living room led into the kitchen. The inside wasn't big, like our beach house. Not that it mattered, but moving around was easy. I spotted two doors that led to other areas of the home, and one was wide open. I could see through it into the bathroom. The other door led into the bedroom.

OH BABY! FUK MI HARD!

36

Gina looked at me and smiled as we stood at the bedroom door. "What do you assume they're doing?" She grabbed my crotch.

"Playing video games." I nodded at the door. "Remain focus."

"Later then, cowboy." Gina winked, and instead of opening the door like a normal person. She kicked it open like we were SWAT. "Ah!" She screamed at the top of her lungs.

What the hell was that? I didn't expect her to yell like a maniac, but it got their attention.

Silva was lying down on the bed, and the woman was riding him cowboy style. I could see a curve in her backside leading down to her bottom, where the covers met, leaving half of her apple-shaped ass exposed. She swiftly launched off Silva and shrieked in a corner on the right side of the bed. I caught a glimpse of her breast (which seemed to be the perfect size for her petite body) before she crossed her arms over her chest.

Suddenly, Silva reached for something under his pillow. I smirked at the ridiculous look on his face when he'd realized what he was searching for wasn't there. I turned my attention to the nightstand next to the bed. A small .22 caliber pistol rested in the open.

"It's on the nightstand," I said serenely.

He froze, realizing what I had said, and looked over at the table.

Gina was close enough by then to stop any threat of being shot. She swiped the gun from the stand with extraordinary speed, leaving Silva without an option to defend himself. "I'll take that." She said with a cunning look in her eyes.

I didn't move an inch. I'd overcome the fear of dying the day I murdered my teacher; life changed for me. Nothing else mattered to me but my goals and if I died trying to achieve them. I'd be ok with that as a settlement.

Silva finally found the courage to look me in the eyes. I saw a terrified man as if a ghost stood in the room behind me. His mouth dropped to the floor, and I felt his energy diminish next to nothing. His bonny chest heaved large amounts of air, showing off his rib cage. His eyes were bloodshot red and low. Smoke clouded the room that could block your vision if your eyes weren't sharp. I spotted a scar across his chest over his heart.

Heart surgery?

The woman trembled in the corner as if she was cold and wasn't sweating a second ago. Her eyes were pinned on me. She didn't blink one time. I was the monster in the room, but what she didn't know, Gina, was the one she needed to be frightened of.

I looked back at Silva. "Do you know who I am?"

It took a moment before I got a response. He was lost, searching for an answer that couldn't be the truth. "Yah man," Silva spoke in a strong Jamaican accent. "A who yuh man? Duppy? A mi fi tell yuh." He paused as if his mind had deceived him. "Jar."

Chapter 9: Rick

I got the location of the cabin from Frankie without getting my head blown off. Mafia guys are not the type of people to second guess about laying you in a coffin. Frankie was no different. Jordan told me a story about him that would send chills down your spine. When Frankie was a small timer, a guy who owed the Don money got put into a tree shredder. That said, the order was given to Frankie. Jordan was there when it happened. He said nothing could be done. The ultimate goal was to bring down the Mob entirely. That guy would have been murdered in prison if not by Frankie. That's the way the world works. Welcome to my life.

I got out of the shower, not ready to start the day. It was a long night. I looked at the prostitute I'd brought to a hotel. I wasn't perfect, and I knew it. I didn't have a wife or kids to come home to after a long day at work to make me feel good. There was no white picket fence with an oversized dog running playfully in the backyard, waiting for his master to throw a ball to fetch.

Her name was Samantha, but her street name was Cherry. The only prostitute I have ever been with, and in another life, I could see her as my wife. That's a bad way to think, considering what she is in this life form. I thought she was gorgeous. She had straight red hair that draped just past her shoulders, long legs that a model would love to work down a runway, tiny breasts that were no bigger than a grapefruit, and an ass that was made to fit perfectly in my hands. Sex with her was amazing, but don't get me wrong; we had an agreement not to get our feelings involved. We talked a lot, and that's what sparked a conversation about life and what we're doing on earth. Things couples spoke about in bed. I had conversations with her that I didn't talk to anyone else about, and she had never been to my place. Maybe that's why I kept coming back to the hotel. I knew she would be there working when I needed someone. I might sound foolish to you, but it's true.

Cherry was still asleep with the sheets barely covering her ass. I thought about another run, but I had to leave. I unclipped five hundred from my bankroll and tossed it on the counter where she could find it. I shook my head as I left the room, locking the door behind me. I sighed in the hallway as two Spanish women (who looked to be in their late forties) passed by, shaking their heads at me. They were cleaners who worked in the hotel. It was regular for them to notice me when I was there. They knew Cherry was a prostitute but didn't realize I was a cop. At first, it bothered me, knowing the two women had to clean up my mess. After a while, not so much. That's probably why I got a nasty look every time I saw them, which was fine by me. I spent five hundred for them to look that way. Call me inconsiderate, but hell, it was well worth to trouble.

I checked my GPS location for the cabin. The ride over was about two hours out. I wasn't in any mood to be driving that far alone, so I stopped by a local coffee shop for a cup of joe and a sausage and cheese bagel. I got the energy needed for the trip. On the way, I thought about the warning Frankie mentioned about Adrian. *If you're not going there to offer a deal on someone's life, watch your own.* I guess you can say that was a thoughtful warning to heed what's ahead. My best bet was to keep a low profile if that's even possible. Jordan and Adrian are both gifted individuals of the same criminal nature. They would see me coming from a mile away. As I got closer to my destination, I thought about the two actually working together as a team. What could I do by myself? I was no match for the likes of them. And from what I had learned about Black Water, he outclassed my rank. I would be dead by dawn.

I parked the car on the side of the road about a half-mile away from the location pinned on the GPS map. If I smoked cigarettes, now would have been the perfect time to spark one. I wished I was back at the hotel with Cherry. Hell, I wouldn't mind spinning the cleaning ladies around the block. I felt anything was better than what I was about to indulge myself in. I did something I don't do much of, and that's pray. I prayed they

42

were not working together. And that when I got to the destination, no one would be there. The cabin would be unoccupied, and I could go home and get some rest. In these times, I would be called a scaredy-cat. And if you saw the expression on my face, it wouldn't seem that way at all, but I was…I was scared for my life and didn't realize it until now.

I came to my senses and got back in the car, ready to ride or die. Whichever came first didn't matter at this stage. I became persisted in capturing Jordan after what I did. My obsession could lead to my downfall, but so could a hooker in a hotel looking for a quick fuck. Anything was possible. I just had to keep my eyes open.

The GPS read *2 mins* until I reached my point. I decided to pull over and walk the rest of the way. I figured it would be safer. I locked the vehicle, bringing nothing but my gun. Frankie was right so far. I was surrounded by woods, and I saw a long dirt road they would surely see me strolling down if I took that route if I was crazy enough to do so. Then again, I could get lost in the woods trying to find the cabin. There could be booby traps for unexpected guests. I thought of several accusations before I decided that taking the woods was my only option.

I journeyed through the wooded area cautiously, watching my back and every step I took. Each sound I heard made me hesitate about proceeding forward. The quiet moments were the worse. It felt like someone was watching, waiting for me to get closer so they could take me by surprise. I couldn't expect Jordan to be here, but Black Water was another thing. This was supposedly his hideout. He would find me, and then you know how the story would end.

Would he torture me, or would it be quick?

I shook the thought of being murdered by a hitman. Suddenly a cabin came slightly into view. I kept my distance; I had gotten as close as I wanted. I scanned the property, and the first thing I noticed was a black Cadillac parked in the driveway. I thought, *what would a fancy car like that be at a place like this?* I considered some type of off-road vehicle would be more appropriate. Nothing more evident from what I could tell came into perspective. Until I saw Jordan exit the cabin. He seemed to be upset about something. I couldn't hear a thing and wanted to test my luck a bit, so I moved closer. I pushed it to the limit, but now I could hear enough to make out a few words.

I fucking hate…I…kill…him…this…Africa by myself…the money…

For the time being, that's all I could understand. *Africa,* I thought. Then I thought about the deal Jordan made with the Africans back at the warehouse. He could still be working with them, trying to get the diamond. I thought about the danger

Kane could be in; what if Jordan went after him? That could turn out to be another problem.

In the next instant, I knew that God didn't answer my prayer. My breath was taken from my lungs without my consent. I felt like I just died when I saw another man emerge from the cabin. *Black Water.* Jordan was indeed working with his brother. *Fuck.* Frankie's words rang out in my mind again.

If you're not going there to offer a deal on someone's life, watch your own.

I wished I could offer a deal on Jordan's life, but it appeared I missed that opportunity. What happened next, I thought, was unimaginable. I saw Mrs. Simmons walk out behind Adrian and what was scary about the circumstances. She didn't appear to be frightened.

Chapter 10: Kane

Big Bruce stood in my doorway. I could not believe my eyes. For a second, I thought I had lost my mind. My eyes started to sting; our staredown was long and hard. At any moment, he could attack without warning. Everything around me became silent as if I was back on the football field running for a touchdown. The other players, coaches, and the crowd felt nonexistent in peak moments. I think people called it tunnel vision.

Finally, I heard Smoke from behind. "Kane," he said.

I felt Smoke's presence, and then I was quickly shoved to the side.

"What's good, my guy?" Smoke said vehemently. "Do we have a problem?"

Smoke looked like cattle in front of Big Bruce. However, there was no fear in his heart. He stood firm and held his ground, ready for whatever would come. Of course, I took down Big Bruce by myself, and there wouldn't be any problem in a four v one situation. Kim would get hers without a doubt, and I would not be able to stop her rage. The heart God gave her was programmed to defend the one she loves, as was I given any other situation that didn't involve hitting a woman. Bear was the strongest person I have ever met in my life. It would take Big Bruce and myself to bring a man of his size to defeat. Big Bruce had shown up at my place, expecting me to be alone. At least that was my assumption. It would take a gun of some sort for him to get out of this predicament.

"Depends on what you wanna do?" Big Bruce said serenely.

Smoke didn't respond. He stayed on guard, waiting for Big Bruce to make a move.

"Who dat?" Bear emerged from the kitchen. He towered over Smoke as he approached the door. He was around the same height as me but packed more muscle. Georgia's best defensive end at a high school level was at the door, asking about my enemy.

"Big Bruce," I said evenly as possible. "The guy I told you about when I was locked up."

"I got this," Bear moved Smoke to the side to stand face to face with Big Bruce. It was amazing how much bigger he looked in comparison. They were the exact height, and the only difference was Big Bruce looked to be the cattle in this standoff.

I kept my attention on Big Bruce and noticed he faltered now a larger man stood at the door. It was three of us, and maybe he realized his chance had diminished.

After a moment of all of us looking crazy at one another, I decided to speak. "Understand you made a mistake by coming here." I moved Bear aside. "Leave, and I won't let my boy break your neck. I don't know how you found this place or why you would come here looking for trouble. I handled you once, and you know I wouldn't hesitate to give you the same treatment. We had our beef in jail. This is the real world. Move on and do something with your life. Trust me. It's the best advice I could give you. If I see you again, it's on sight." I began to shut the door in his face, but what Big Bruce said next shocked me in a way that affected me emotionally.

"T-Mac is dead," Bruce said. "I wanted you –"

Big Bruce didn't get the chance to finish his last statement. I grabbed him by the neck and commenced to choke the life out of him. We fell outside of the house onto the front porch. We wrestled around on the ground as if we were back in jail, continuing our legendry battle in the cafeteria. I threw a few good blows to his rib cage, and I felt returned licks to mines. His shots were more potent than before as if he wouldn't get any stronger after I left. Like, he had trained for this moment all his life, and when the time came, he was more than prepared. It felt like he snapped a bone with each direct hit. I could only pray he felt the same, and somehow I would prevail a second time.

"You murdered my friend," I spit a combination of dirt and blood from my mouth. "You sonofvabitch!" I roared. Bear and Smoke was on us within a matter of seconds. There was no way they could interfere without hitting me. Big Bruce and I were locked together like two UFC fighters going for a submission. I didn't expect anything less. "Ah!" I reluctantly released my grip—an excruciating amount of pain struck my stab wound. It felt fresh as if Abel had stabbed me again in the very same spot. Big Bruce gain the advantage after that point. If my boys had not been there to help, I would have been dead. I felt about two hundred and eighty pounds of body weight removed from over me. The kind of feeling you got when you lost weight. I rolled over on my side, holding the wound. A thick liquid soaked through my shirt. *Blood,* I thought. The stitches were damaged in the fight. A cloud of dirt momentary blocked my vision. When it became clear, I saw Bear and Smoke whaling on Big Bruce. He didn't stand a chance. Bear dealt the most damage, from what I could tell. I had to give it to Bruce. He tried his best to fight back, but Bear's powerful blows seemed to be overwhelming.

"What are you idiots doing!" Out of nowhere, I heard Kim yelling at the top of her lungs. "Are you trying to get the police called on us? What type of neighborhood do y'all think this is?"

Her words froze everyone like she had cast a spell of stillness. I managed to sit up on my butt. Bear, Smoke, and even Big Bruce didn't respond. It was like we were more scared of fighting with her than each other. "Why are you here causing trouble?" she walked straight to Bruce and got in his face. She looked like a small child having a fit in front of her father. That's how massive he appeared next to her. When Bruce didn't respond, she surprisingly slapped him hard enough for the sound to echo down the street.

Kim had shocked us all, and I tried to get on my feet, but with no luck, I could not. I thought Big Bruce was about to rip her a new asshole. Shockingly, he didn't move one bit. Maybe because there wasn't anything he could do about it with us on standby, and he didn't appear affected by it. To him, it probably felt like being slapped by a baby. Bear nor did Smoke reacted. It could be they were waiting for Bruce to bust a move that never happened.

Instead, he said without contempt. "I came here to let Kane know a guard murdered his friend T-Mac." He looked at me. I could see he was serious. "He started it, Miss lady. I know we had problems when we were locked up. But, after you left. T-Mac and I became friends after a few months. My mother had passed. I caused a lot of people trouble. I sank in a dark place, and T-Mac somehow found away in his heart to actually give a damn what was wrong. We talked a few times in my cell and in the yard. Hell, he got a job in the kitchen and used to slid food to me inmates couldn't get. He's the first person I spoke with while I was in. Just when I found a friend, he was killed. That guard had it out for em. Funny how shit changes with a couple of words."

"Get the fuck outta here," I said. "No way he would ever befriend you." Kim came to my aid and tried to help me stand. Bear saw what was going on and came over to handle the load. I was back on my feet with my arm around my friend for support.

"Believe what you want." Suddenly, he reached in his pocket.

"Hold up, playboy," Smoke was on Bruce in an instant, responding faster than a late-night booty call. He lifted his shirt, showing off a shiny piece of chrome that could hit harder than any of us. Smoke was about that life. I watched him dropped a kid from whom we were purchasing guns. The kid wasn't a threat, and still, Smoke put em down.

Big Bruce ceased all movement. I supposed he got the message. "Chill," he said. "I have a letter from T-Mac and wanted to make sure you got it. He didn't get the chance to mail it before he died. I found it on the table in his cell. It's the least I could do for T-Mac."

Bruce looked over at me, and I nodded for him to proceed. Smoke kept his hand under his shirt as a precaution. Bruce slowly reached in his pocket and revealed a folded envelope. He cautiously walked over and handed it to me before stepping back with his hands held high.

I read the handwriting on the front. It was addressed to this location. That's how Big Bruce found out where I live.

Kane Simmons from your boy T-Mac.

It was definitely T-Mac's handwriting. "He's telling the truth," I told them and slit open the letter.

Kane,

Hey man, how is it going out there in the real world? I can't wait to leave this place and hangout. Man, my lawyer said there is a chance the judge will knock some time off my fifteen-year sentence if I'm a good boy and if I can complete counseling without any alarming signs. We'll see how that goes. The good thing about all this is Big Bruce, and I kinda became friends. I still don't trust em, but he's been nice so far. I know it sounds crazy, but the guy needed somebody to talk to. Just like I did when I met you. And no, I'm not insane, or neither did he force me to write this. His mother had a heart attack and died. I was eating breakfast when I found out. The guy had been on mute for a month, and at first, I didn't want to concern myself, but something inside of me wouldn't allow that to happen. I walked past his cell and heard em cryin. Yeah, he was cryin like a baby. I thought he had got fifteen years instead of me. He told me what happened, and ever since, we have been on good terms. He even fought off a guard who had been given me problems, saying I'll be somebody's sweet lil pink pussy when I get down the road. The guy wouldn't stop, and he even shoved me on several occasions. One day, Big Bruce punched him square in the face. It was shocking he did that for me. He got sent to the hole, and the judge added three more months to his sentence. He spent two weeks in there before he made it back to the dorm. Yeah, he did that for me. KRAZY I tell you, but it happened. Anyway, I need a girl to talk to on the outside. Does your girl have any pretty friends? Hook me up. Also, thanks for the money, big dawg. It meant a lot. Well, I don't want to hold you, so I'll talk to you later. PEACE…

P.S. I got a job working in the kitchen. Now I can eat all the cereal I want!

Your boy, T-Mac

Chapter 11: Kim

"Let's get him inside before he bleeds to death," I said. I was more concerned about Kane than having the police called on us for disturbing the peace. I wrapped my arm around his waist with Bear's support on the other side. Smoke opened the door for us. I turned to the gorilla the boys were fighting with and said. "You too."

He looked perplexed as if he didn't speak English.

"Yes," I said sincerely. "I'm talking to you, big fella."

"Hell nah, sis." Smoke responded vehemently. "This the mufuc–"

"Did I asked you?" I interrupted with a serious look on my face. "I don't care what problems y'all have. He came here to deliver a message in good faith, and y'all jump him. Look at what y'all did to his face. His lip and eye got busted pretty good." I looked at Bear when I mentioned his bruises. "I'm gonna fix him up because I don't think he has adequate health insurance after just being released. Am I right?"

The guy shook his head no. "I don't want to cause any trouble. I'll be on my way."

"Good," Smoke said.

"Shut up, Smoke," I said. "Do you want me to stop cooking for you?"

"Man," Smoke sighed. "Why you gotta be that way?"

"It's cool," Kane spoke up. "He can come in. His face swells pretty bad. Trust me, I know. Let her fix em up. He did me a solid by delivering the letter, and from what I read. That's good enough for me."

"I'm cool with it," Bear said. "I need someone my size I can arm wrestle wit. I'm tired of whoopin Smoke's ass." He joked.

"Then it's settled," I said. "Let's get inside before I kick all of your asses."

"Thank you, Miss lady." The guy said respectfully.

"This some fuck shit." I heard Smoke mutter.

"Smoke," I warned.

"A'ight, sis," Smoke said submissively. "My bad."

We stepped inside the house, and Smoke locked the door. Of course, he would be the last the enter. I figured he wanted to keep a close eye on the big guy. I didn't see a problem with Smoke being concerned about Kane. I knew how he felt about him as well as myself. His feelings for us run deep, and after his grandmother died, we became the only family members he has left in his mind. Like a lion protecting his pack, that's my brother until the end. That's why I love him.

"Let's get him on the couch," I told Bear. We hauled Kane over to the sofa. He groaned a bit, and the expression on his face screamed agony. I hated Abel more than anyone alive for the pain he caused us. All of this is because of him and that

55

crooked cop. The Planner or whoever he claims to be. I hate him just the same.

"Smoke," I looked at him. "I need a lighter, scissors, and some bandages for Kane while I keep pressure on his wound. Bear grabbed an ice pack from the kitchen and gave it to our friend over here for his face. We need to stop the swelling on his eye." I was ready to get to work. A room full of muscle, but no one knew how to treat themselves after an injury. I should have gone to school and became a doctor. I found myself patching more wounds on these guys than an actual surgent. I should feel special, but I didn't; it was something I had to do to keep us safe and alive. With what's been going on around us lately, my services were a requirement. And I kind of enjoy taking care of my boys.

Bear tossed the ice pack to the guy. "Yo." He alerted him as the pack soared through the air.

He caught it with one hand. "Thanks." He placed it over his eye.

"What's your name?" I asked.

"Bruce," he said. He sat on the sofa chair next to the fireplace.

"So Bruce," I noticed how enormous he was sitting in the chair. I could barely see it under his body mass. If Bear had not been around, I'm not sure if I would have let Bruce inside. He looked a bit scary, not in a terrifying way, but more like an oversized super-soldier created in a laboratory. "Why didn't you just mail the letter yourself instead of coming here?" It was a question I had to ask. It was clear to me how he had got here. He used the address on the letter. Especially, knowing if you show up expectedly, a fight could breakout. That seemed peculiar to me, no matter how you frame it.

"That's what the hell I want to know," Smoke said as he came downstairs with the supplies. He handed them to me. "Shit, don't sit right wit me."

Bruce appeared to search for the right words before opening his mouth. His lip was now the size of an almond. "Honestly, T-Mac used to speak about Kane as if he was the best person in the world. At first, it got to me because of our history. But after a while, I saw things differently. Most of the advice he gave me came from you. The same way you helped him, that information helped me. I wanted to fuck you up after our fight. No lie, I had never gone toe to toe with someone and lost. I was always superior until...you. After mom, man, I tell you. I was fucked up. And then...T-Mac. All I had was the damn letter. I did think about mailing it on a few occasions. Shid, I even thought about throwing it away. The longer I held on to it, the more I thought of T-Mac and the things he would say about you. I guess I wanted to found out for myself."

57

"Nigga," Smoke erupted. "Ain't nobody tryin to be your friend."

"Stop it, Smoke." I said. "That's enough." I turned to Bruce as I worked on Kane's wound. "That's thoughtful of you, Bruce. Since the first day I met Kane, I've been in love, and these guys will tell you the same. He's precisely what T-Mac said he was. I'm sorry about your mother and T-Mac. I can't tell Kane how to feel about you. That's up to him, but I feel the sincerity in your heart. I'm willing to give you a chance."

"Same," Bear added. "Fuck it."

I looked at Smoke.

"Man..." he began and sighed. "Kane is my best friend; note that. I'll fuck you up if you ever play em or not true to what you say. I'm already on edge wit the shit that had been going on lately. We can't afford any more distractions. You feel me? Kane says, you good...you good wit me. But, I'll never trust you."

Bruce nodded at Smoke. "I don't blame you."

Everyone focused on Kane, waiting for an answer.

After a long minute of silence, he said. "We'll talk."

A sign of relief came across Bruce's face. I smirked on the inside, knowing what I had done would benefit the crew later. I knew exactly who Bruce was the moment I saw him at the door. I even watched them give it to him in the front before I interfered. He deserved it. I thought of it as an initiation. I don't give two cents about Bruce and how he felt. It's a war sharping between our crew and Abel's. We need all of the muscle we can get. Bruce could be the perfect soldier if used correctly. Another Bear doesn't hurt. My only concern was protecting Kane and what happened to Redd affected us all. Bruce would be his replacement. I could not tell the guys that because they wouldn't understand without duking it out at the time. My intentions might have been a little cruel, but that's life. You have to learn how to adapt to any circumstance. All I had to do was keep Smoke from killing Bruce until Abel was dead and after I got that out of him. Smoke could take care of Bruce however he pleased, and I wouldn't have a care in the world after he was gone.

Chapter 12: Abel

I looked back at Silva. "Do you know who I am?"

It took a moment before I got a response. He was lost, searching for an answer that couldn't be the truth. "Yah man," Silva spoke in a strong Jamaican accent. "A who yuh man? Duppy? A mi fi tell yuh." He paused as if his mind had deceived him. "Jar."

I looked at Gina. "He thinks I'm a ghost." That was the first time in my life someone called me Jar or even thought I resembled him with a bald head. I thought it was amusing coming from Silva. That had to be some good weed.

Gina had a grin on her face, paying more attention to the woman crying in the corner. "Can I play with her?" She asked like a kid meeting their future best friend for the first time.

"Kiss mi neck," Silva was surprised. He looked at Gina. "Ah weh dat come fram? Wah di bumboclaat."

"He's offended," I told Gina. "Maybe later." Silva's eyes shifted from Gina to me. A bit of confusion spread across his face. "Don't worry. I won't let her touch your yamhead. From my understanding, that's what she is, right?"

"Yuh tink mi lagga head?" Silva said. "Shi wifey."

"I don't think you're stupid," I told him. "In fact, I think you're a smart man who knows how to make money."

Silva adjusted on the bed. A spark ignited in his eyes when I mentioned money. "Mi G, wah yuh waah?"

"Let me properly introduce myself," I acknowledged with a slight head nod. "My name is Abel, former son of Jar." Silva's low red eyes grew to the size of a grape. Even his wife stopped crying and paid attention after my last words. "I'm here to offer you a deal, and I'm fully aware you used to fly for Jar. I want you to continue your services with me. As of right now, you're in debt with Jar. He paid you yearly, and the year isn't quite over. You see...after he died, you would assume that it was free money. But, now I'm in charge...that debt is owed to me." I paused to give him a moment to process the information. "Take me to Africa along with my crew. We'll use the same route you usually take to reach Libya. You know the place. No guns to smuggle, so no danger of getting caught. Your cargo will be us. I'll clear your debt once we safely arrive. If you choose not to accept my offer –"

BOOM!

Gina had shot the pistol and hit the back wall, barely missing Silva's head.

"Wah di bumboclaat!" Silva flinched and put his arms over his head as if to protect himself. "Yuh try to queng mi!"

I gave Gina a look like, are you trying to mess this up?

"Sorry," Gina laughed at her own stupidity, but I knew she wouldn't risk killing him. "I couldn't help myself."

I turned my attention back to Silva. "I need an answer before she kills you." I used it as a scare tactic even though I didn't have to. The damage was already done. *You might as well feed the beast.*

"Yuh, man." Silva kept his hands over his head. He didn't bother looking up when he replied. "Mi wuk, yuh addi baas."

"Good, that's what I wanted to hear." I turned around and faced the door. I didn't leave immediately. There was something else I had to do to make sure Silva stayed true to his word. "Be ready to depart tonight. Your wife will remain with us until then…Gina."

"Wah di rass!" Silva spat.

I heard Gina forcing Silva's wife to obey my demands. The woman began crying for Silva to do something about it.

"How di bloodclaat yuh fi duh mi like dat!" The woman cried, directing her words at Silva.

"Mi luv," Silva said.

"What's your name, beautiful?" Gina asked sarcastically and pushed the woman through the door. The woman had put on a cut-off shirt and booty shorts.

"She'll be fine," I told Silva without turning around. "When the plane is ready, meet back here. Turn on the porch light to signify you're done." I didn't wait for a response. He could do what I asked or leave his wife in Gina's hands. And from what I could tell, Gina might want a sample while we waited. I grinned at that...she did look tempting. *What a nice little snack.* "You better hurry."

Chapter 13: Jordan

"I fucking hate that piece of shit," I said, pacing back and forth in front of the cabin. "I should kill him. I can do this on my own. Go to Africa by myself and get the money." I contemplated taking on the job with just me and Mrs. Simmons. I couldn't do it without her, and she wouldn't give up the information to save her life. That stubborn woman would be the death of me.

I heard the door shut, and I turned around to see who followed me outside. Adrian and Mrs. Simmons were on the porch standing there watching me throw a fit like a five-year-old. My temper flared the more I thought about what Adrian said to me in the cabin. What did he know about family legacy? I'm the reason he was able to continue under the radar. And what I get for it? A contract on my head for my efforts to save his ass.

Mrs. Simmons gaze narrowed on me as if she had something sneaky up her sleeve. Maybe I was getting paranoid about being a wanted man by the feds. Or perhaps it could be The Planner screwing with my mind. But something didn't sit right, and that was the cop in me feeling that uneasiness. I'd thought embracing being a bad guy would be simple. Apparently, it's not. I'm wanted, Adrian could do me in, and then there's Mrs. Simmons deceitful ass and her mistrustful looks, and I can't forget the fucking Africans. What the hell was I doing here in the first place? Kane should have been my main priority.

That was the plan. He got my money, and I should have settled for that.

Mrs. Simmons stepped off the porch and approached me. Adrian stayed put, watching from a distance. "I need you to focus." She said. "If we are to get through this alive. I need you here with me."

I waited to answer, thinking about what I should do with myself. I peered over to Adrian, and his sullen face didn't frighten me one bit. A grimace expression showed on my face that I couldn't hide, and I said through clenched teeth. "Ok." As if it was the most challenging thing I'd ever done.

Mrs. Simmons smiled at me. I felt a chill emit from her heart. It was evident because it was warm out. I heard stories about women from the Caribbean and the powers they possess over men. I wondered if this was another case. She – the proprietary of my soul. "Good," she said. Her eyes veered to the side of my head. "Don't look. Someone is watching us from the woods."

Fuck. The Feds. That was my first thought. They found me, and the speed at which they did was shocking. How long had they been on my trail was questionable. Since the hospital or maybe the Don's car had a tracking device on it from previous stakeouts. We could be surrounded by cops, and I wouldn't have known if it wasn't for Mrs. Simmons.

I looked up to see if Adrian spotted the opposition. To my astonishment, he was gone. As I mentioned before, you don't show up here without him aware of you. My ill-temper got the best of me, and I dropped my guard. I scanned the rest of the area without moving. I didn't spot anyone. This could be a solo act, but why would anyone attempt coming here by themselves? The level of danger was a GTA five-star rating. There was a low chance of escaping alive, and someone was brave enough to risk their life.

I swiftly turned around, trying to catch the person off-guard. Fuck what Mrs. Simmons said about not looking. If I wanted a fucking bullet in the back of my head, that would have been an excellent idea. I shifted from the FBI to another hitman with a contract on my life. Adrian didn't complete the job. That meant someone could still want me dead.

Adrian had already captured the perpetrator. It was hard to make out who the lunatic was from a distance. Adrian had the guy in an armlock from behind and walked him in our direction. The guy didn't put up a fight. He must have known his time had come. He was good as dead. I could make out a few details as they approached—a white guy, curly blonde hair, with an unorthodox walk, came into view.

Get the fuck outta here, I thought.

I smiled. "Holy shit," I murmured. For a second, I thought my mind had played a trick on me, or I saw a face on a different person I desired to kill. But no, it was Rick in the flesh. The same goofy white guy who used to ride shotgun in my car. The same guy I had to look after fresh out of the training facility. At that moment, my blood began to simmer, thinking about what he did—the same guy who used Kane to set me up and ruin my career. *White boy Rick,* I thought. *You don't know how dead you are, rookie.*

Adrian stopped with Rick right in front of me. "How's it going, rook?" Somehow I controlled myself from putting a bullet between his eyes. But that wouldn't be enough for Rick or...enough for me.

"Jordan," Rick said with sarcasm in his voice. "How's life?"

"Better than yours right now." I snarled.

"You two know each other?" Adrian asked.

"Yeah," I answered. "I used to babysit this punk."

"More like I took care of your old ass." Rick countered.

"Partners," Adrian's eyes flickered between Rick and me. "This is interesting."

"I knew if anybody could track me down, it would be you." I praised him. He kept his attention on me the whole time as I spoke. "You're a smart guy, Rick. But without my help, you're not street smart. Coming here alone was suicide. Did you show up alone...without anybody to back you?"

Rick didn't make a sound. I could feel his temerity leave his body.

Like my boy, *Bill Duke* said in *Menace II Society.* "You know you don' fuck up, right? You know you fuck up." I always wanted to say that line but never got the perfect opportunity.

"We should get him inside and find out what he knows," Adrian said.

"No," My eyes pierced through Rick and struck Adrian. "We should finish him before he becomes a problem." I took my gun out of the holster and put it to Rick's tempo.

"Wait," Mrs. Simmons spoke up. "We should find out what he knows. It's better to keep him alive until we depart in case something goes wrong. If he found us, there could be others. It'd be best we have a bargaining chip."

"So you're with them, Mrs. Simmons?" Rick said, incredulously, as if he came to that conclusion beforehand. "What about your sons? What would they think?"

"You mean, son," Mrs. Simmons had a rawness in her tone. "Kane is the only child I have, detective."

Chapter 14: Kane

Kim finished attending to my wound. I'd reopened the stitches fighting with Big Bruce. Luckily, my boys were around to help, or I would have possibly died. That's how bad, big boy (who was now sitting on my couch) punctured the wound. It hurt like hell. I couldn't turn to either side without making an ugly grimace on my face, and Big Bruce didn't look pretty either. His face had swelled just as I'd expected. I thought he could have applied for the monster in the eighties horror movie *Pumpkinhead.* Bear went to work on Bruce, and I'd missed the good part because my face was in the damn dirt for the majority of the fight. Call it a sick fantasy, but I thought it would be fascinating to observe the two gorillas fight. Even though I knew Bear would come out victorious. And the ice pack Bruce held on his face said it all. I bet Big Bruce felt more like Little Bruce after experiencing Bear's extraordinary strength.

"I think it'd be best if I get some rest and you guys sort things out," Kim said and stood up to leave us. "Hopefully, when I come back down, I won't have to play, doctor." She kissed me on the forehead like I was her child getting ready for school. "Later," she said to everyone and left.

Nobody spoke for a hot minute. We were locked in on Big Bruce, and he was locked in on us. Time would tell how this uncomfortable situation would play out. After what we been through while incarcerated, how could he just calmly sit there thinking he was safe? That was the most intriguing thought that came to mind. He was a different man I'd never seen before today. You could scrap with your best friend over something and find yourselves sitting in the living room, having a cold one and laughing about what had happened. Similar to this situation, but it wasn't my best friend. He was standing with a contemptuous look on his face, ready to pop off. This guy was my enemy, or at least I thought he was twenty minutes ago when he was driving blows to my rib cage. It's hard to trust anybody after what Abel did to me. And now I found myself opening up to someone else I'm not sure of. My mother said I have a heart made of gold, but today…I wish that wasn't true.

"Don't overthink it," Smoke said, breaking the eerie silence in the room. "You're good, Brucie boy. Sis saved your life today, but I wouldn't count on it being that way mañana."

Big Bruce maintained his composure. "Right," he said sarcastically. He turned to Bear. "That's one hell of a punch you got. More potent than your man's." Bruce looked at me.

"I wish you could've smiled when you said that," I shot back. "Anyway, when did you get out? I thought you would get a life sentence for being so ugly."

"Ha," Bear started laughing.

Smoke kept a straight face. It didn't seem to amuse him in the slightest.

Big Bruce made a sound that seemed to be an attempt to laugh. "That was a good one." He moved the ice pack from his face. "I got out two days ago. Time served, no papers, I'm clear. The same as you."

"The same as me." I mocked. "You didn't think about visiting your family before coming here to get your ass kicked?" I tried to study his face. My father told me to keep a close eye on my enemies, and this was as close as it gets. My enemy was literally sitting on my living room sofa, having a conversation with me.

"I don't have anybody who cares enough about me." Big Bruce said and placed the ice pack over his eye again. "My mother was all I had. Never met my father tho, but I heard he was something special."

"What do you mean by special?" I asked.

"My mother told me he was a boxer," Big Bruce said. "he abandoned us when I was born. I guess his career was more important."

"What was his name?" I asked. I found myself intrigued by Bruce's story. Growing up without knowing or ever meeting your real dad had to be rough. I can't imagine if my father wasn't there for me. He taught me everything I know. When I discovered Abel was the one who murdered him, it changed my life.

"Don't know," Bruce murmured.

"Den how you know this nigga used to box?" Smoke asked. "My guy, your aura is shacky as fuck." He turned to me. "You hear this guy?"

Big Bruce stood. "You wanna find out?"

"Hell yeah, nigga." Smoke got in Bruce's face. "Ain't nobody scared of you punk ass."

Bear somehow beat Smoke to Big Bruce. It was the fastest I'd ever seen him move. He stood in the middle of the two men. "Bruh, you know what Kim said."

"Fuck dat," Smoke said truculently. "He shouldn't be here, and you know that, Bear. He's our enemy."

"You're saying that as if I'd murdered somebody." Surprisingly, Big Bruce backed off. "Me and your man got in one fight. Stop acting like I tried to kill the nigga. We were in jail, but you might be too soft to know anything about that besides visiting your boy like a hoe."

Those words cut deep in Smoke's pride. Bruce was right about Smoke. He has never been locked up in his life. After being jailed for a long time, you pretty much could tell who'd serve some time. It's like a new sense you gain once reactivated into the world.

72

"Let's find out what it's like since him a hoe." Smoke reached under his shirt. A click-clack sound came next.

"Yo," I stood as fast as my body would allow. I felt like an old man struggling up from a wheelchair. I put my hand on the barrel and forced him to lower it. "You want us to go down for murder because you're in your feelings." I looked Smoke in the eyes. "C'mon, you're better than that, than him. You know what we're about. Let it ride. He did me a favor. Respect him for that, at the least."

Smoke sighed and tucked the gun under his shirt. "I need a blunt." Smoke left out of the house into the backyard.

"Don't worry," Bear said. "That's his way of saying you're right. He'll be good after burning one."

"I know," I said in a murmur. *But what if he ain't,* I thought.

Chapter 15: Abel

Gina nudged the woman through the front door, and I followed behind them. After I secured the door, I spotted Snake sitting on the couch watching TV. He had a banana in his hand and a cup of milk. The same thing he had for breakfast every morning.

"Who's the chick?" Snake took a sip from the cup.

"Some girl we picked up at the bar in town." Gina joked. She guided the woman through the living room. "Have a seat here, next to me, sweet thang." The woman did as Gina instructed. They were sitting together on the loveseat.

Snake sighed. "Don't insult my intelligence." Gina gave him a grin, and he turned to me. "Who is she, and why didn't I know you two were leaving the house? You could've got me."

"Silva's wife," I told him. "She'll be with us until the plane is ready. It was no big deal, so I didn't bother to wake you. We have a long day ahead of us, and you needed to rest. You're coming off a concussion, and I need that big brain of yours operating at full capability." Snake's face said he understood my intentions for leaving him behind. Bear had knocked his lights out. The blow was powerful enough to kill him. He got lucky, and I mean lucky–he didn't die right there on the spot.

"That big guy put you to sleep like a baby," Gina said, and it didn't sound disbelieving. "Moma shoulda popped her tittie out and gave you some milk." She laughed. "You know you like milk."

Snake sucked his teeth. "Shut up," he looked furious, but it was true.

"Give him a break," I said and then looked at the woman. "What's your name?"

She didn't respond. Her eyes flickered back and forth between us, contemplating if she was in danger. Probably, wondering if she would make it out of this alive if Silva didn't come through. Almost a sense of mistrust streamed off her body.

"No one will harm a hair on your head," I told her. "Relax, you're going to be with us for a while."

"Yeah, I'll protect you." Gina licked the side of the woman's face, and she moved in disgust. "Um…tasty."

"I think you're going crazy." Snake said, looking at Gina.

"Maybe," Gina answered, unfazed by the comment. "Do you want to find out?"

Before Snake could respond, Bam walked into the room. "I thought I was the only one who felt that way." He eyed Gina.

"What, gay?" Gina smiled at Bam. "You've never been with a woman. Let alone two." She played with the woman's hair, twirling it around with her index finger. The woman seemed too afraid to move.

"I've been with a woman," Bam said through clenched teeth.

"Sure you have," Gina responded. "That's why you're acting so uptight."

"Do I need to remind you two what our goal is?" I said, trying to ease the tension before things got out of hand.

Bam eyed Gina before turning his attention to me. He sighed, knowing he would never get the last word. "Who is Gina's new pet?"

"Sliva's bae," Gina spoke up.

Bam gave Gina a look that said, *I didn't ask you.*

"So, do you have a name or not?" I asked evenly.

The woman looked at me and finally answered. "Britt."

"Like, Brittany?" Bam asked.

"Like, Brittany." Gina mocked. "Lame."

"I'm growing sick of your mockery," Bam growled.

"Then, hopefully, you'll die," Gina replied.

"Bitch," Bam muttered.

"Quiet," I erupted. "You two are working my last nerve." My attention was on the woman. "Britt, if you need anything while you're here, let me know. I'll make sure you're taken care of."

"Thank you," Britt said in a whisper.

"Well then," I felt my body growing weak from not getting proper rest. I was up all night waiting for Silva to return. Now that things were somewhat in order, I needed a few hours for my body to recover. "I'll be upstairs if anybody needs me." I didn't want to tell them how tired I was because there could be trouble between Gina and Bam. In the back of my mind, I knew one of them would make a move on the other if I weren't aware. I needed both of them to be on the same page for now.

I didn't show any signs of being tired as I left the room. Nobody said a word, and I made my way upstairs to the bedroom. I shut the door behind me and put my ear to the door. I didn't hear a sound, not even a peep from Gina or Bam. That was good. I sat down on the bed and kicked off my shoes. The others were unaware I was mentally and physically drained from the fight I had with Kane. I wanted to appear as if everything was fine, but it wasn't. Gina didn't even know how I felt. Kane's fists felt hard as cement. My bones ached, and they felt broken. I was spitting up blood for a week. I've been dealing with the pain without any medical attention. I could only imagine the pain Snake was in after that knucklehead knocked him into another galaxy. It was the first time I'd ever heard Gina cry the way she did for my safety. In this condition, if Kane and I were to fight again, he would defeat me with ease. I got the diamond, so there was no need to engage with him once more. Even though he's a knucklehead, he was an extremely strong knucklehead.

Suddenly, there was a knock at the door. *Gina,* I thought, *coming to soothe me.* I could use her company, so I slowly got

77

up and walked to the door. My right arm was wrapped around my rib cage like a body bandage. As I approached the door, I fixed my posture to hide the pain I was in. I stood straight and firm as I opened the door. "Gina," I spoke too soon. It wasn't Gina standing in the doorway, nor was it Bam, coming to complain about her. Snake would've been my best guess after those options.

"Can I come in?" Britt's voice was somehow soothing.

I looked around for Gina, puzzled that she wasn't there beside her. I sighed, "Sure."

Chapter 16: Rick

"So you're with them, Mrs. Simmons?" I said, incredulously. I'd come to that conclusion beforehand after witnessing how settled she seemed to be around two murderous men. "What about your sons? What would they think?" Abel and Kane were on bad terms. I could have told her, but I wanted to see the expression on her face when I mentioned them both as nothing was wrong.

"You mean, son," Mrs. Simmons sounded very serious. "Kane is the only child I have, detective."

Whoa, I thought. *That's interesting.* She didn't consider Abel as her son. Mrs. Simmons couldn't possibly know anything about their fight unless Kane said something to her. Abel's name wasn't in the news either. As of right now, the kid was in the clear. Yes, there was something more profound than their fight, something she knew that I didn't. But why Jordan if she's on Kane's side? Could they be working together to bring Jordan and Abel down?

"Why would you say that, Mrs. Simmons?" I needed an answer, and before I could get one, I was shoved in the back by Adrian.

"C'mon," Adrian gave me a hard push toward the cabin. "that's enough questions for now."

I stumbled forward a bit and quickly regained my footing. I stared at Mrs. Simmons as I passed by and didn't sense any fear whatsoever in her eyes. How could this be with everything that has happened to her? I was there the day her husband was shot and killed in his office. I was the one who did an extensive background check on their family. She was not the woman I'd profiled a few months ago who checked in a mental institution.

I approached the cabin and noticed that every window had dirt smudge over it so that you couldn't see inside. The porch was dry; no life at all, not even a chair to behold the view. Black Water, or should I say, Adrian, got the door without taking his eyes off me. I passed by him into the cabin. The inside was immaculate. Every piece of furniture looked new. I noticed a family picture above the fireplace. A man and two boys. Jordan, Adrian, and perhaps their father. I thought that it was odd a woman wasn't in the portrait. There was something else I couldn't quite put my finger on. The man in the photo looked familiar, and there was no way I'd met him before. But…it felt that way.

Adrian guided me to the couch next to a table with a book on it, *The Bourne Ultimatum.* I figured it belonged to Adrian. A little ironic if you asked me. I sat down and couldn't help to notice how comfortable the sofa felt. I could have fallen asleep if I wasn't with two men who could put me that way for good. I may never see the light of day again. This could be my last ride. What would Jason Bourne do in this situation? Probably die because some writer put all of his moves in a book.

"Watch em," Adrian said before he left the room.

I felt a sense of urgency. My body tightened up, not knowing what would come next. I rather keep Adrian in my field of view than have him off somewhere doing God knows what. And even that wouldn't be good enough. When I was watching him from the woods. Adrian went from the porch to surprising me from behind. He was more like a fucking ninja than a hitman.

Jordan sat in a rocking chair next to the fireplace. He kept his eyes on me without saying a word as if he was trying to read my mind. Mrs. Simmons sat next to me, and that didn't shock me until she said, "What do you know about Kane? Is he ok?"

I kept my mouth shut. It's a tactic I learned back at the training facility. People don't respond well to silence. Especially if it was a question regarding somebody they care about. That much told me she hadn't crossed over entirely.

"That's a wonderful idea," Jordan leaned forward in the chair. "Tell us about my good ol' buddy, Kane. How's he doing? Rich, I bet."

My eyes shifted from Jordan back to Mrs. Simmons. There was a question that needed to be answered before anything. "Why are you working with them? What can Jordan do for you that we can't? I watched the footage in the hospital. Jordan kidnapped you – that I know much. But, you're here and calm as day as if you planned your kidnapping. What the fuck is going on?"

Mrs. Simmons looked down at her hands. She fiddled with her fingers, nervously. A bit of concern showed on her face. She sighed and pulled herself back together. I saw a spark in her eyes I'd not seen before, like a jolt of assurance and confidence sprouted from nowhere. Her next words were sharp and dangerously constructed like an infrared-homing missile. "I don't work for them. They work for me, detective."

Chapter 17: Kane

My situation couldn't get any worse, I thought ironically. Abel, The Planner, maybe the Africans, and now Big Bruce were all perhaps out to finish me off for good. I was still trying to process T- Mac's death. I looked down at my cell phone, wishing I would receive a call from Gwinnett County Detention Center, and it would be the operator saying, you have a collect call from T- Mac. But I didn't get a call, and my friend was very much dead.

I brought my attention up from the phone. Bear and Big Bruce were the only ones left sitting in the living room with me. I'd got a feeling that Bear actually liked having another big guy around. Bear was undoubtedly the monster in the room, but Bruce was right there, muscle-wise. True, I'm a bit taller, but Bruce outweighed me by at least thirty pounds. "You *know* I have to go take care of some business," I looked at Bear when I spoke. He acknowledged me with a head nod. "Stay here with him until I get back." I signaled at Bruce. "I'll take Smoke with me so he can get some fresh air and talk to him about what we have here. Maybe I can calm his nerves."

"Sounds like a plan," Bear said. "I'm good," and eyed me. Meaning to say, *I won't fall asleep on the job.*

That's what I needed to hear, even though I had a good feeling he wouldn't. Ever since his therapy sessions, he'd been good, like he said. I'd monitored his progress over the past month, and he still fell asleep every now and then, but mainly when he had absolutely nothing to do. Kim was my main concern, and Bear would be the perfect bodyguard. I couldn't fight off a fly in this condition, and Smoke would more than likely put a bullet in Bruce's head if something went down. Bear proved he was much stronger than Bruce, so I figured Bruce didn't want those problems while banged up. Plus, I honestly thought he needed a friend. Let's see if he's able to be trustworthy.

"I won't be a problem," Big Bruce sounded sincere. "This guy is straight out of a comic book. Your boy is tougher than the Hulk." He looked at Bear. "What you say your name was again?"

"Bear," he said with a chuckle.

"Bear," Bruce repeated. "That's fitting for a guy your size. Whatchu throwing up?"

"Four-fifty," Bear said with pride.

"Damn," Bruce awed. "I just maxed out at four before I got out." He looked at me. "Where you at, tough guy?"

"Three-fifty," I said and stood.

"What," Big Bruce looked shocked. "And I let you kick my ass," he muttered.

"More determination than strength," I said.

"That'll do it," Bear chimed in.

"A'ight," I said. "We'll be back in an hour. Play nice and try not to break each other necks." I left them up to the challenge and walked out onto the back patio. When I opened the back door, I instantly smelled Kush in the air. It was that potent, what we called that loud pack.

I stood next to Smoke. We didn't look at each other. He acknowledged I was there but kept his eyes focused on our new friend. I looked in the same direction at the dog I'd broken. He was looking back at us, preferably me—the guy who caused his pain.

"You really fucked em up," Smoke said in a low voice. He had a fat one rolled and puffed out a cloud of smoke. You would've thought a train went by.

That was all he said at the time. Big Bruce fucked with his nerves by showing up; this was his way of releasing some stress. "Yeah, I did. And now I feel sorry about it." I went along with the subject, trying to avoid bringing up Big Bruce. I knew how Smoke got when something irritating was on his mind. Talking about it would only frustrate him even more. Moving his mind from the problem for a bit usually brought him back. I learned that over time. He would open up when he settled down like always.

"Why," he asked. "He would've bitten a chunk of your ass off." He held the blunt out to me. "Look at em. He looks vicious even with a damn cone around his neck."

I took the blunt, and I know I shouldn't have, but I did. Maybe it was because of Smoke or Bruce being here, or perhaps I thought it would ease the pain I was in. Whatever the case, I took it and put it to my mouth, and inhaled, thinking about his question. "Honestly, I don't know. I never had a dog and always wondered what it would be like to have one. I've known that dog longer than you. I remember when he was a puppy, watching him from my window running around back there. I was twelve when I first met him. He grew up in front of my eyes. He didn't seem like a vicious dog as he got bigger. I even stuck my hand through the fence one day, and he licked it. After Kim and I returned from the hospital, I watched him, and he watched me." I passed the blunt and blow out smoke. "I thought about the two years I was gone. Maybe he forgot who I was, and that's why he attacked me when I jumped into his backyard. He was only protecting his territory from someone he didn't know as we do, like the way you are now."

Smoke sighed. He knew what I was getting at. He was protecting me from Big Bruce, just like the dog was protecting his owners from me. A person he saw as a threat to his family. It's only natural for someone to protect the ones they love by

86

any means necessary. That's life. I couldn't fault the dog, Smoke, or anybody for that matter. After my father passed, I'd learned it's kill or be killed. This is a crazy world, and sometimes, that's the only way to survive in it.

"You know that's why I fuck with you," he blew out a chain of smoke. "You see things differently. Your mind operates on a level that perceives the world for what it truly is. I wish I could see shit the way you do, but until then...I got you, my friend."

"One hunnid," I said. We watched the dog and smoked the blunt down halfway. "We need to visit Tang and find out if he learned any new information about Abel."

"We already know he murdered your father," Smoke put the blunt out and placed it in a small steel case and slipped it in his pocket. "What else can there be?"

"Maybe a plan or something," I said. "Abel makes plans for everything he does. I thought there could be a slight chance he created one for murdering our father. I know about the smuggling business and all that, but that's not Abel. He's different; there has to be something else."

"If there is," Smoke began. "I'm sure Tang found it. It's been a month, and he told us a day. I should've picked up the laptop when you were in the hospital."

"Nah, it's cool," I said. "You were more concerned about my life, and that's a good enough reason for it to slip your mind. It would've slipped my mind too if it were you. In any case, I thought we should head over and see what's good."

"What about–"

"Bear got it," that's all I had to say.

"Forsho," he responded and didn't sound angry about it. "I'm fucked up. You have to drive, big homie."

"My guy," I called after Smoke. "I'm fucked up too." He didn't hear me because he'd already left the patio.

I parked the Humvee in front of Tang Technologies, and we got out.

"That's a nice little gift you got from the Africans," Smoke signaled at the Humvee. "Shid, once we're able to spend that bread we got, I'm getting one just like it. But, I'm slammin' 32' rims on my shit, black on black, limo tint, and ten 15' subs in the back. That hoe gon beat!" he got excited, thinking about what he could do with the money we got from the Africans. It's true. We were sitting on millions we couldn't spend just yet.

"My father's Ferrari should be arriving soon. It comes out this year." I said. "I'll be happy with that for a while."

"Didn't he have to purchase it ahead of time?" he asked.

"Yeah," I said. "You had to be on a list or some shit."

"Damn," he awed, "Lucky ass, you're gettin' some exclusive shit."

I opened the door for us, and we entered the building. Nothing had changed. The inside looked the same. A bunch of people who appeared to be nerds or geniuses walked around, checking out the cool technology the place has to offer. I spotted Robo Babe and kept my distance to frame from embarrassment like the last time. After about thirty seconds, Tang emerged from the back to greet us.

"What's good, my nig–"

"Stop yourself right there before I bust your head," I said.

"My bad, my G." Tang apologized. "My new girl slang, affecting the way I talk."

"Well, she bout to affect this ass whoppin' you're about to catch if you say that word," I said.

"She black?" Smoke asked, interested to know.

Smoke didn't let the N-word affect him coming from none blacks as it did me. Plus, he was too high to care.

"With a fat ass, my G." Tang emphasized. He used a hand motion to show how big it was.

"Damn," Smoke said with wide eyes. "nigga you lying, her ass ain't that fat."

"You better believe it," Tang said. "She got a donkey back there."

They laughed.

"Yo," I interrupted their boy chat. "What's up with the laptop? Did you find anything?"

"This guy," Tang said. "Always about business. How do you put up with him? He doesn't watch football on Sundays?"

"Ol' shit," Smoke said with a closed fist covering his mouth. "You shouldn't have said that."

By the time Smoke finished his last statement. I had lifted Tang off his feet into the air like I was holding a baby high over my head. "You make one more racist comment, and I'm gonna rip your head off and put it up your ass. You'll be the one walking around with a donkey back there. You feel me?"

"I feel you, I feel you, my G." Tang was scared and probably thought I would kill him right there in the store. "Please, I don't wanna badonkadonk. I don't want guys slappin' my ass." He cried. "Especially, big black du-" he stopped and looked at my face. "Never mind, just please don't hurt me, my G. Smoke, tell em I'm cool, please."

"I thought you said you could whoop Kane's ass?" Smoke said with sarcasm.

"I didn't say that," Tang cried. "You know I wouldn't dare." His eyes looked toward the ground. "Fuck man, I never been this high up, and I'm afraid of heights, my G. I feel my legs getting numb. I'm about to pass out." He dangled his feet like a child on a swing set."

"Stop being overdramatic," Smoke started laughing. "People are beginning to look." He told me. "Thugs are in the house. You feel me."

I glanced around the area. People were watching me manhandle Tang, and he owned the place. I wasn't going to hurt him. I just wanted him to understand I'm not the one to play with.

"Ok," he squeaked out. "your brother is planning to take over the government. He's on some black market shit, and I wasn't trying to be racist when I said black."

I released Tang, and he fell to the floor like a hand puppet. "My neck, my back...my neck, and my back." He quoted Ezel from the movie Friday.

"This is the best high moment I've ever had." Smoke laughed. "Get up, pimp." He helped Tang to his feet.

"What do you mean, take over the government?" I asked skeptically.

Chapter 18: Abel

"Can I come in?" Britt's voice was somehow soothing.

I looked around for Gina, puzzled that she wasn't there beside her. I sighed, "Sure."

I let out a breath of air, sighing if I should shut the door or not. If Gina found out Britt and I are in the room alone, there wouldn't be a good outcome for any of us in the house. This was crossing the line. Gina already expressed her love for me as I did with her. There was no way Gina knew about this. I decided not to shut the door, but I did leave enough space for someone to look inside without worry. However, you couldn't see the bed from the outside of the room.

Britt stood in the center of the room. I walked past her and sat on the edge of the bed. She didn't appear frightened of me. She looked calmer than before. Her arms were crossed over her breast, covering them from my view even though she had on a shirt. My eyes felt like they were about ten pounds heavier. At any second, I could pass out from exhaustion. I managed to look her in the eyes. I didn't notice before that they were a light hazel brown—no signs of makeup either, not one blemish on her facial features. Not even a light spot, and her face was the same color as her body, certifying a perfect full-body tan. I didn't want to imagine if her private area obtained the same color or if it was smoothly shaven the way I like it. I shook the thought from my mind. My heart belonged to one woman now, Gina. She was my equal. "Is there something I can do for you?"

She broke eye contact and aimed her sights at the floor. "I...I didn't feel comfortable around them." She said. "The woman, Gina. She seems like a very mean person. I don't think I like her much. The way she touches me doesn't feel right. I've never been with another woman before. And the others keep staring at my body. Mostly at my breast like they'd never been with a woman." She got tense. "I...just feel like I'm safe around you. Is it ok if I stay in here with you?"

I thought about it for a moment. Gina told me before she wouldn't mind experiencing a threesome with another woman and myself. Britt was absolutely stunning, and that could provoke Gina's hunger to make a move on her. Snake and Bam have never been with a woman built like Britt. They're considered nerds, and nerds don't achieve popularity in school over jocks until later in life when they're filthy rich. I could see how they might be intimating toward Britt, having a staring problem like a predator lurking for the perfect opportunity. I'd done a horrible thing to a woman that I now regret. I wanted Kane to hurt, and I knew that would crush his soul. I'd never considered what it would do to her, how it would affect her spirit. If that were to happen to Gina, I wouldn't know what to do but seek revenge.

93

"How did you get away from Gina?" That intrigued me the most. "Did you tell her you were coming up?"

"No," she looked up. "I told her I needed to use the restroom. She stood by the door for a while, but she eventually left. That's when I came here. Are you two together?"

Her question took me by surprise. We didn't give off any signs of being involved around Britt. Gina must have mentioned something to her, not that it mattered to me. "Why would a married woman asked if we're in a relationship?" I adjusted on the bed, feeling my body weakening as time passed.

"Silva is not my husband," she assured. "He wants to get married but–"

"You don't feel like he's the right man for you." I couldn't help but hold the area over my rib cage that caused pain in my chest.

"Yes," she looked up at me with those beautiful eyes, and I almost turned away. "The sex is good and all, but I don't see a future with him. I hate flying for one, and that's his job. He's a runner. And the time we spend together only consists of weed and sex. I want a man who has power, a man like..." She looked away from me. "A man who can provide a good life for me. I want to feel like a queen."

"Why are you opening up all of a sudden," I asked. "you're telling me this after I took you hostage?"

94

She eyed me again, and I saw a flare in them that I hadn't seen before. "I...don't know. Honestly, when you came into the room and took control over Sliva the way you did. Kinda felt sexy. I was scared at first, not knowing if you would kill me. You had the power, and Sliva was...Sliva. I can't marry a guy like that. And ever since I've been around you, you have been nothing short of nice to me. You're a large man, and you appear to be intelligent. I'm a sapiosexual, and that why I find myself attracted to you."

Suddenly, the door flew open and slammed against the wall. I thought it would come off the hinges. Gina stormed into the room, and she looked furious. She stood behind Britt. "Well, don't be, honey. He's mine!"

As soon as Britt turned around, Gina knocked her out with a closed fist to the face. The shot sounded like thunder after it connected her jaw.

I looked at Britt sprawled out on the floor, out cold. Gina was standing over her like Laila Ali, posing like her father. I brought my attention to her. "Was that necessary?"

Chapter 19: Jordan

"I don't work for them." Mrs. Simmons had a serious look on her face. "They work for me, detective."

What she said was shocking. Why would Rick believe she was in control of two highly wanted criminals? I searched for a valid reason in my soul that said she wasn't trying to convince Rick we were in cahoots. If she was, what then? Would he still arrest her for being involved in criminal activity? Of course, he would. She'd be a terrorist just like the two of us. Like…Abel. The son she disowns, that…hideous monster of a child she created with the dead man. For now, I thought, I'll let Mrs. Simmons convince Rick she was the leader of our operation. It'd look good in the papers if we were apprehended. I'd tell the media it was all her plan. She'd been the mastermind who brought all this together. I didn't kill anyone at the warehouse when Rick busted in on us, and he doesn't know how I got the diamond in the first place. Unless Kane mentioned something to him, that was a risk I was willing to live with. I would be free from public humility. I was a good cop who deep undercover without letting his peers know about it. That would be my comeback, my story of salvation.

The look on Rick's face made me want to cry. His scrunched-up face was the ugliest expression I'd ever witnessed in my life. It was legendary. It was a face a father made when his fourteen-year-old daughter came home and said she was pregnant by an older man. "What do you mean?"

I smirked. "What do you think she means, idiot?" I leaned back in the chair. The wood was beginning to make my ass hurt. *How did my old man sit in this thing for so damn long?* "As she said, we work for her. It's that simple." I added to what was already weighing on his mind—the thought of us three working together.

Rick looked at me with a flare in his eyes. "What did you do to her?" He turned to Mrs. Simmons. "Did he put you up to this by threatening you?"

I began laughing. "Threaten her? If you only know the type of shit this woman has put me through. And we thought her husband's secret was massive. She's on another level. I would say she provoke him into becoming a smuggler."

I looked at Mrs. Simmons. I'd thought she would object to what I was spilling out of my dirty mouth. She put her head down as if she was ashamed because it was true.

"Mrs. Simmons," Rick's voice was soft and caring in an incredulous tone. "What is he saying?"

Mrs. Simmons didn't respond, so I took the opportunity to add value to my cause even though I would kill him later on. "She's playing us millions to fly to Africa where her dead husband has a safe-house full of cash and guns. His

97

headquarters." I paused to enjoy the shocked look on Rick's ugly face. "That's right...she's a monster." I hoped he felt the huge grin on my face as a sign of fuck you right up the ass. I wanted Rick to know our plan. He would die anyway, so it didn't matter any. I fancied him knowing I'd outsmarted him once again. Me–The Planner, baby.

"What the hell are you doing!" Adrian came back into the room full of rage. "Why would you tell him what we have planned." He looked at Mrs. Simmons and shook his head.

"Because he's gonna die anyway!" I stood infuriated. The Planner took over. "You shouldn't come at me that way if you want to keep breathing, brother! I don't care if we're working together. That can all end, right here, right now." I ball my fists as if I was an anima character powering up. It felt good to let off some steam.

"How do you know he's not bugged?" Adrian sighed, calming himself down before I dealt with him. "Did you search him?" I didn't think about it, and he saw the look on my face confirming it. "And you're supposed to be a cop." I was caught up in my feelings to notice Adrian holding rope and duct tape. He tossed the supplies at me, and I caught only the tape. The rope dropped at my feet. "Do you know what to do with that?"

"Of course I do," I said through clenched teeth.

"Stand," Adrian told Rick. "and take off all of your clothes."

98

"No," Rick said. "that's absurd. I won't disrespect Mrs. Simmons."

I glanced at Mrs. Simmons. Her head was still facing her lap. My attention went back on Adrian, moving toward Rick.

In one swift motion that my eyes could barely capture, Adrian somehow held Rick by his Adam's apple with two fingers. Rick appeared to be struggling to breathe. His face began to turn dark purple. He tried to fight Adrian off, but his blows weren't effective enough. I'd never seen anything like this before now. I hate to admit it, but Adrian was a trained killer whose skills were superior to mine.

"I have hold of your thyroid cartilage," Adian's voice was dark. "I can easily crush your larynx, protecting your vocal cords. You would never be able to speak again." He paused, and the expression on Rick's face was enough to frighten me. "And that's only the make of it. I could damage your trachea just enough for you to slowly drown in your own blood. Those are your options if you do not obey me from this point on." He released Rick, and he fell to his knees, holding his neck and gasping for air. "Can you please take off your clothes?" He asked nicely as if what just took place never happened.

I could see blood returning to Rick's face as he regained air in his lungs. I was so scared that I wanted to make sure I had bullets in my gun but now wasn't the time. Rick made it back to his feet and began with his overcoat, then his shirt, pants, and underwear fell to the floor. Adrian reached in his pocket and revealed a tiny device that he used to scan Rick's entire body. He was searching for a tracking device. He then picked up Rick's clothes and burned them in the fireplace.

"There," Adrian said. "No one will come looking for you." He walked over to the door and picked up a bag, then tossed it to Rick. "Put on these clothes."

Rick did what he was told without saying a single word. He groaned as he got dressed, assuring me of the pain Adrian caused to his neck.

"You'll be able to speak again in an hour or two," Adrian said. "Depending on how strong your throat is. That's how long it will take for the swelling to go down. A second longer, and you would've died. I could judge by the color on your face. You're pretty tough. Typically, guys your size would pass out in the first thirty seconds. Then again, I could be getting weak." He laughed as if it were funny. "I still have a few questions for you. I'll make some hot tea for your throat to speed up the process."

Way to go, I thought. *He's a fucking nurse too.*

Chapter 20: Kane

"What do you mean, take over the government?" I asked skeptically.

Tang was bent over, holding his knees and gasping for air like he just finished running a mile.

"What are you doing," I said incredulously. "You're acting like I choked the hell out of you."

"I...–" he started, then continued panting. "Anxiety attack. I get like this when gangsta shit happens."

"Gangsta shit," Smoke said sarcastically. "What gangsta shit? The man literally picked you up and sat you back down without harming a hair on your Lil' Asian head, pimp."

"Yeah," Tang said. "I thought y'all would beat my ass old school style to initiate me into the crew. I guessed wrong, so this is how they do it now." He finally stood like he was a hero in a movie. "I made it through that shit. I'm tough as nails. I told you, Smoke." He held out his hand. "Where's my flag?"

"Flag?" Smoke asked.

"Our gang colors," Tang said seriously. "I'm bout to rep to the fullest."

I shook my head from side to side. This guy was a mess. I had to come up with something since I did tell him he was a part of our crew, but I didn't think he thought gang-related. To get the information out of him about Abel, I played along. "Man, we don't use flags anymore. Dat shit old, plus it'll get you shot in the wrong hood."

He looked at Smoke with a confused look on his face. "How do I rep the crew?"

Tang had high-hopes to be a part of our crew since high school. I didn't desire to break his spirit by telling him we weren't that type of crew. I could see the look in his eyes that it would destroy him if he couldn't represent the crew. I did the only thing I could think of at the time. "Smoke, tell 'em how we rep the crew?"

"Um..." Smoke looked at me because he didn't have an answer either. I shot a look back like you made me drive, remember? You're up. "Jordans."

"What?" Tang asked, disbelieving. "Jordans?"

"Hell yeah," Smoke said. "A fresh pair of Jordans will get a nigga murk. Look at what's on my feet and Kane's. We both got on J's. That's how we rep the crew."

"By wearing a fresh pair of Jordans?" Tang looked at me for confirmation.

I sighed on the inside. It was better than anything I could come up with, so I agreed. "Jordans." I held out my left shoe and rotated my foot, showing off my black, orange, and tan *Jordan Retro 1 High OG Shattered Backboard.* "The more expensive they are, the harder you rep."

"Them the OG's," Tang awed. "They're like fo hunnid. Them bitches hard!" He looked at Smoke's shoes. "Jordan Retro 1 Fearless Chicago's." His eyes shifted between the two of us like a kid looking at Christmas gifts the night before. "When do I get mine?"

"What size do you wear?" I asked.

"Seven," he answered excitedly.

I cracked a smile, and so did Smoke.

"What?" His smile disappeared.

"Nothing," I replied. I refused to tell him he had a small shoe size for a guy. It would possibly damage his pride, knowing him. "That's a hard size to find, but I know a sneakerhead who can find exclusives in any size and colorway. I'll get him to send you a pair of the Toko Bio Hack's."

"No fucking way," Tang put his hand over his mouth and shed a tear. "I always wanted a pair of those." He suddenly hugged me. "Thank you, my G."

I looked at Smoke and muttered. "Look at what you got me into."

He had a big grin on his face and shrugged his shoulders, not expecting Tang to bust out in tears over a pair of shoes.

Tang released me. "I'm not crying," he whipped his face. "Those tears are from being up all night doing gang shit, my G."

"Cool," I said sarcastically. "Now explain to me what you meant by Abel taking over the government?"

Tang gathered himself before speaking. "I found information about securing funds in a Swiss bank account, places he wants to travel, world leaders to convey of his importance, members of elite foreign families, mafia personal in the UK, and Irland, and…a plan to murder your father so he could take over his out of country business contacts in Asia, South America, and Africa."

My heart dropped to the fucking floor. Tang provided more than enough intel on Abel and his plan. That's what this whole thing was about, power. Abel thought he was smart enough to take over the world at such a young age. He figured murdering our father would give him a jump start toward that goal. I didn't expect this like I didn't expect my father's demise at the hands of flesh and blood. My so-called brother had carved out a plan to be a criminal mastermind like…The Planner. I couldn't respond to Tang. The information hit hard. "Thank you," was all I could manage to say. "Let's go, Smoke."

"What about the laptop," Tang asked.

"Was that everything you could find?" I asked.

"Everything, my G." Tang responded.

I thought about how the intel on the laptop could harm our family name. It wasn't only about what it could do to Abel, but my father. And the damage it would cause my mother if the FBI connected her to him as a conspirator. It didn't take much for me to decide what to do. "Then destroy it."

Chapter: 21 Abel

"Was that necessary?" I asked Gina. A girl fight was not what I needed. Britt expressed how she felt about me, and Gina overheard the conversation. In any other circumstance, Gina would have every right to knock Britt lights out. It wasn't the time to get in a fight over feelings. At least that's what I thought. Gina was different when I first met her. Being around me unlocked something inside of her, a fire in her soul that ignited once we fell in love. She desired to be my right side, my everything, and no one would stop her. Another woman falling for me was new to Gina. Another problem she would fix if need be. That's part of the reason I fell for her. I knew she would be by my side, even if it meant death.

Gina stared into my eyes. "What were you two talking about?" I could see for the first time veins bulging in her forehead.

"Nothing important," I told her the truth.

"It didn't sound like nothing," Gina kicked Britt in the side. The blow had enough force to flip Britt to the opposite side she was lying on.

"Gina," I said, trying not to show any emotion for Britt. The woman was out already, but Gina didn't care. At the same time, I wasn't going to defend Britt. That would only ignite a more extensive fire under Gina. "I only care for one woman, you. She snuck in here when you left her side. I answered the door, thinking you were coming up to be with me. That's why I left it open, so you wouldn't think there was something between us. I didn't know she had feelings for me. I just found out, the same as you, my love." I stood, and an unexpected pain shot through my body, causing me to fold a bit and wrap my arm around my waist.

"Are you all right," I heard a sensitive tone in Gina's voice.

"I'm fine," I straightened up, trying to stand firm for her. I sighed and looked into her eyes. There was a concerned expression on her face. "Don't worry."

"Is it from the fight?" Gina asked. She stepped over Britt as if she wasn't there, the person who really needed attention. Gina held me by the shoulders. "Your ribs are bruised, aren't they?"

"Yes, but they're not broken," I said.

"It's been weeks, and you have been dealing with this without telling me?" She asked worriedly.

"I didn't want to concern you with minor problems," I told her. "We have more important things to worry about."

"But you need medical attention," She rubbed the sides of my shoulders. "How bad does it hurt?"

"Not that bad," I lied. It hurt like hell, and it didn't feel like it was getting better. I thought if I got some rest and didn't work my body as much, everything would be fine. A man of my stature should have healed in a week or two. It seems Kane was stronger than I'd expected.

Gina did something that I wasn't prepared for; she poked the lower right side of my rib cage.

I grimaced as she applied pressure with a single finger. It felt like she had the strength of ten men in her index finger. The kind of power you see exhibited in kung fu movies. I reacted by backing away in agony, just enough to relieve her affliction.

"See," Gina stepped in to close the distance between us. "You can't go on like this. Your ribs might not be broken, but you are in pain. It wouldn't be a good idea to seek medical attention at a hospital. Have you at least tried to treat it on your own?"

"Yes," I assured her. "Every night, when you all are asleep, I use an icepack. I thought it would have healed by now."

"You need to lay down," she guided me to the bed. "I'll take care of everything from here on out until you're yourself again. Don't worry about anything, my love. When we get to Africa, we'll find a doctor to look you over."

She was prepared for the unknown. She instantly knew what to do. That's why there couldn't be another, only her. "Thank you," I said and closed my eyes. "I need you to focus and don't get caught up with Bam or Britt. You're my eyes, ears, heart, and soul. Never forget that, Gina." I opened my eyes for a short moment. I saw a tear roll down her cheek. I felt the same energy from her I felt in my father's office when she'd brought me a sandwich. No matter how tough she is on the outside, on the inside, my words affected her like any other woman in love. "One more thing."

"Anything, my love."

"Don't leave Britt on the floor," I asked, and her face instantly reverted to hate. "If you decide to leave the room." I smiled.

Gina's evil looked turned back into a warm smile. She laid in the bed beside me and gently rested her head on my massive shoulder, opting to leave Britt on the floor.

Chapter 22: Rick

My throat was in an extreme amount of pain. After I put on the clothes, I sat back down next to Mrs. Simmons. I was lost and didn't know what to do with myself. Adrian could kill me in an instant. I was prey to him. A sitting duck, if you want to call it that. I tried messaging the pain I wasn't accustomed to, but any amount of pressure caused it to ache worse. Speaking was not an option. Adrian said it would take at least two hours before I could talk. All I could do was drink the tea and wait until my vocal cords heal. *Why did I pick today to become a hero?* The question lingered in my mind as I sat there waiting for Adrian– for Black Water.

I looked up and saw an odd expression on Jordan's face. It was a look that I have never seen on anyone. His eyes were wide, and his jaw appeared to drop down to his chest. He would have given a scream mask competition for the best horrific look on Halloween. His face was that scary. I wondered if he even knew how he looked at the time. What Adrian did to me must have shaken him.

I turned to Mrs. Simmons, and she didn't appear to be surprised at all. Her head was down in the same position as before the incident with Adrian. Perhaps she missed the entire thing? Then again, nothing to me was surprising about this woman anymore. What she'd told me was more devastating than what happened to me. I knew what Adrian was capable of but not her. I would've never guessed she was working with them if she hadn't told me. And for some odd reason, I didn't want to believe a word she said, but deep down, I knew her words were true.

Adrian walked into the room with tea after about ten minutes. I could see the stream coming from the cup as he entered. I thought he'd poisoned it, but why when he could've killed me a second ago? There was a reason I was alive. He needed me for something but what? His moves were very calculated, not offbeat like Jordan's. Jordan was like an action hero when I worked with him, and from what I could tell, Adrian was that and then some. He was the bad guy at the end of the game you died against until the fiftieth try. And in real life, you only get one life. I was on number two.

I felt the heat from the cup when it reached my hands. Adrian walked over to the fireplace after giving it to me. I wanted to say thank you, but for what? The man nearly killed me, and I should thank him for bringing me tea? My mother preached every day about having good manners. I guessed they stuck with me even through bad times. I took a sip of the tea and couldn't help to notice how good it was. I felt a flow of heat travel down my throat, creating a path of warmth until it hit my stomach. I glanced at Jordan, and he grimaced back like he was anticipating my death after I'd took the first sip. If I could smile, I would have just to piss him off—the bastard.

Adrian spoke up, "we have to take him with us." It was short and sweet.

"What!" Jordan erupted.

Mrs. Simmons looked up for the first time we spoke but remained silent. I could see in her eyes she disapproved.

Adrian was quiet with his back turned to us.

"Are you fucking insane?" Jordan continued. "Say something, you idiot!"

I sipped the tea, thinking it was an excellent idea. Hell, I didn't want to die here, not helpless like this. Now I had a chance to plan an escape. I wasn't gonna die, not just yet. I kept my eyes on Jordan to see if he would look at me. If Black Water wanted to keep me alive, then Jordan would want me dead. They were opposite, and that's the way Jordan seemed to like it. He disagreed with everything Adrian said, starting with the incident outside of the cabin. Jordan was out there fussing at himself about something. I got a feeling I was about to find out.

Jordan was Adrian's shadow. He stood and got directly behind the man without fearing for his life. "He's fucking smarter than you think. I worked with him for years. I know how he operates. He'll plan an escape and ruin our plans. Is that what you wish to happen? You want to spend the rest of your life in the feds?" He paused, panting like a wildman. "You asshole, say something!" Another minute went by, and Jordan turned to Mrs. Simmons. "This wasn't a good idea. We need to leave."

Mrs. Simmons didn't say anything. She stared at Jordan aimlessly.

"Have you fucking gone crazy too," Jordan balled his right fist. "Shit!"

"You're not going anywhere," Adrian finally spoke. "calm down and stop bickering." He grabbed a file off the mantle of the fireplace and handed it to Jordan. "You came here because you need someone to fly you to Africa."

Africa, I thought. *Why would Mrs. Simmons want to fly to Africa with Jordan when she could safely fly commercial? Are they in some kind of relationship? Wait, she said they work for her. Fuck.*

I realized what they were after. When I worked on her husband's case, I discovered he was a smuggler, a high-end warlord of some kind. Maybe she desired to continue his business, and Jordan was the only way to achieve that through connections without alarming the FBI.

Jordan's had a shocked look on his face after reading the file. "Fuck," he muttered. "The plan is being held at the police impound. How the fuck did you manage for that to happen?"

"Does it matter?" Adrian turned around to face Jordan. "Our only concern is getting inside the impound without being noticed."

"That's why we need Rick," he snarled. Jordan's eyes wandered over to me. He had to wait to kill me, and the fact he had to work with me again was a gunshot to his heart. I could tell that much by the look on his face. He reminded me of a pit bull whose leash wasn't long enough to reach his food as if to tease him.

"The plane was seized after a job," Adrian said. "That's all you need to know. We'll use Rick to get us inside to get it back. There isn't any other way. I'm sure you know how difficult a task it would be without an agent. Instead of flying under the radar, we'll fly legit, using his credentials to evade air traffic controllers. It'll be more secure with an officer on board and faster."

I had to admit, Adrian came up with a hell of a plan. He could use me to get the plane and fly without air traffic controllers causing problems. FBI agents could do things of the sort without a hassle. The only problem would be fueling the plan at a landing strip without being noticed. The three of them would have to hide and trust me not to report them. Jordan would never allow me to handle such a task without some type of security blanket.

"Ok," Jordan agreed. "we'll go along with your plan, but first, we have to secure our safety." Jordan looked at me. "I told you this guy was smart. He'll try to give us up the first chance he gets. I followed Rick around before I went rogue. I wanted to see what the rookie was about. It seems he does have a weakness for a hooker."

Cherry, I thought. I saw an evil grin spread across Jordan's face.

"I think I'll have someone pay Samantha Higgins a visit while we're in the air," Jordan said.

Chapter 23: Kane

We left Tang Technologies and headed back to the house. I let Smoke drive the Humvee on the way back. I was too messed up in the head to focus on the road. We stayed quiet halfway through the trip until he broke the silence.

"Don't worry yourself, my guy," Smoke said.

I was looking out of the window. My mind was somewhere in La La Land. I glanced over at him, and his eyes were straightforward. "I can't help it. My mother is out there somewhere with a manic, and Lord knows what he's doing to her. I figured he would've contacted me by now. It's been over a month. What if he killed her because of me? I wouldn't know what to do with myself."

"Don't think that way," Smoke's eyes shifted from the road to me then back to the road. "I can see it on your face. Remember, you were hospitalized when it happened. I'm sure that through his plan for a loop, not able to contact you. I bet his ass is hiding out, waiting for your release. Your mother is fine. He can't do anything without her. We know how he thinks. He'll want to make a deal for the diamond."

"A diamond I don't have," I reminded him.

"He doesn't know that," Smoke reassured me. "All we need is a location. The rest is up in the air. You know how we get down." I saw a smile form on the side of his mouth.

I thought about what he'd said. The Planner is smart, and he would be a fool to touch her, knowing how I would respond if something happened to her. That wouldn't be wise if he wants the diamond. He initially learned how to find me, and it shouldn't be a problem to find me a second time. "I feel like shit because I let her down. I was supposed to protect her, and I failed to do that...the same with Kim." I hung my head down toward my lap. The fact I couldn't do anything about it worried me.

"Hey," Smoke raised his voice. "tighten up. That wasn't your fault. I feel just as bad about what happened to sis. I had to go through that with you. We got her back, and we'll do the same with mom. She's like a mother to me. I feel the same; she treated us like brothers. I know shit is fucked up right now, but we'll get back right. I need you to keep a straight head. You're the brains, and that's the only way this will work. I know Abel is out there doing God knows what. We'll get at him another time. Right now, we need to be ready for The Planner."

I sighed. "I don't know what I would do without you," I said. "What Tang told us fucked up my head. I was thinking about all the shit Abel had done. Where the fuck did I go wrong with that kid? I don't know, man, he never saw me as a brother. My whole life, I'd treated him fairly. I understand our father treated me slightly differently. That's because I walked in his shadow. And it really wasn't his fault. It was the people around him. I

117

looked at Abel as he was the special one. I mean, he's smart as fuck. I wished I were the one blessed to be a genius. I always thought he was the lucky one. And yet, he wasn't smart enough to care about me. He took our father regardless of how our mother would feel about it. That sonofvabitch made her have a mental breakdown. All over some black market shit. He's just as responsible as The Planner." I balled my fist so tight my knuckles turned white.

"I can't possibly know how you feel," Smoke said as he pulled into the driveway. He stopped the truck in front of the house. "One thing I can promise you. I'll be there no matter the circumstances. Whatever happens to you will happen to me first. After my G Ma passed, I thought it was the end for me. But you and sis brought me back. I realized I still have people who care about my black ass. I didn't realize how much I meant to you guys until that day sis was..." he paused, and I thought he would shed a tear, but he didn't. "Fuck, I hate thinking about it. It's us against them. As you get older, you start to understand who your real friends are, and those friends eventually become your new family. I didn't understand what my G Ma meant when she first said that to me. Now I know. Your friends know more about you than your family through longevity, I guess...experience. That's what I think she was trying to tell me.

When we face Abel again, we'll face him as family, and he'll be our enemy."

"Fuckin' right we will," I smiled and held out my hand, and he gave me some dap. We got out of the Humvee and walked into the house.

"Yo!" I yelled through the house. Bear stood as we entered the living room. He was sitting on the couch playing NFL Madden with Big Bruce.

"What's good," Bear said, still focused on the television screen. "Bruh…" he threw his hands up.

Smoke sat down by the table and pulled out his strap, and placed the weapon on it, still in arms reached. He didn't show any signs of being unhappy about Big Bruce being around, and it didn't deliver on his face.

I looked at the screen. The Falcons vs. Saints, and it was a tie game. I already knew Bear had the Falcons. He's a huge Atlanta fan and selects them every time he picked up the sticks. "You're a Saints fan," I asked Big Bruce.

"Hell nah," he responded with his eyes locked on the screen. "he beat me to the Falcons, so it's only right I beat his ass with the Saints."

I couldn't help but smile. "Seems like you two were having a good time while we were out."

119

"This nigga cold," Bear said. "he beat my ass the first game."

"Wha.." I was shocked because Bear never lost in Madden. That's his game. "Oh yeah, what was the score?"

"38 to 17," Big Bruce spoke up.

"Damn, like that?" I said, amazed. I sat down next to Smoke on the sofa.

"It was like that," Bear said. "Ingram ran all over my ass for 231 yards. I got his ass on lock this game tho."

I would have never thought Big Bruce was a Madden fan. With an attitude like his, who the fuck would want to play with him? I suppose you don't know someone until you spend time around them. So far, Bruce was turning out to be alright. The game was 21 to 21, with thirty seconds left on the clock. Big Bruce had the ball on the forty-yard line on Bear's side of the field. He was preparing to kick a field goal; Bruce ran the clock down to five seconds and then hiked the ball. Bear user picked a cornerback and blitzed the kicker.

"Ol' shit!" Smoke surprisingly erupted. "Run that shit, my guy!"

Bear blocked the kick and picked up the ball. I stood out of my seat, just as excited as Smoke. The time had expired. Bruce was on Bear's ass with a player who was fast as hell. He hawked Bear down and tackled him right before the endzone.

120

Bear used the truck stick to drag the player into the endzone for a touchdown.

"That's what the fuck I'm talkin' 'bout!" Bear roared excitedly.

"My nigga," Smoke and Bear slapped hands. "Don't ever let a nigga come into our house and win at our game."

"Good shit," Big Bruce said and gave Bear some dap.

"That was a fire-ass ending," I said. "But I want you both to know y'all can't fuck with me."

We all laughed, and I have to admit. It felt good even with Big Bruce there, the person who I looked at as an enemy. It's funny what a video game could bring people together. I went back in time when it was Redd instead of Bruce. No doubt, Bruce would never replace him, but it was like the gap Redd left behind was momentarily filled. I looked around the room, and everyone appeared to be happy. This was what I needed to take my mind off The Planner and Abel. Eventually, I would have to get back focus. A few hours later, I got a call, and it wasn't a radio voice telling me the conditions to get my mother home safe. Instead, it was Rick…and he sounded scared.

Chapter 24: Abel

Gina and I didn't get the opportunity to make love. The pain was too great in my chest. What she did with her hands, tongue, and mouth was another story. She knew how to get me aroused over and over again. Her head bobbed up and down for an hour until I fell asleep. I tried not to make a sound while Britt was down for the count on the floor. I enjoyed every second of Gina's throat and wished I could return the same pleasure. She didn't mind that I was unable to perform. I'm a broken man who couldn't satisfy a woman's simple needs. When I'm healthy, I'll return the sensation ten times over.

I slowly sat up and propped my back against the headboard. I looked down at Gina, and she was sound asleep. I caressed her hair gently with my left hand. Over the past two months, she'd let it grow out from the close-cut style she used to sport. We have to keep a low profile with everything that happened from the museum to the hospital job. I suggested that she grow her hair, partly because I desired to see how she would look with it long. She didn't like it at first until the day I guided my fingers through it. She loved the feeling, and it grew on her.

Britt was still on the floor. It shocked me that she was out for so long. It has been five hours since the altercation. I had to do something about her being on the floor. I couldn't leave her there like that for some reason. I'd been close to my mother all of my life until the incident with her husband. People thought of me as a momma's boy. It was something I couldn't shake no matter how hard I tried. She was there to baby me when times got rough; when Kane would go off with Jar, and when I couldn't exceed at something I worked at vigorously–she was there for me. I hated that a woman had to look after me when I was trying to become a man...like Jar.

I eased Gina to the side without waking her. I crept from the bed with caution. If Gina caught me trying to help Britt, all hell would break loose. I shook my head, unaware of how to feel. The first thing I did was scoop Britt's head into my hands. There was a bruise about the size of a small rock you would skid across a lake. The damage was done to her jaw on the right side of her face, and it had turned a dark reddish-purple color. I rested her head in my arms and lifted her with ease. She felt about 120, about half my size.

Britt's eyes flickered open and shut as she regained consciousness. "What happened?" she asked, disoriented.

I shushed her. The last thing I would wish for is to wake Gina. "Be quiet," I turned for the door. Britt seemed to regain some focus. She moved a bit in my arms and smiled up at me. At that very moment, I heard some commotion coming from behind me. I knew it was Gina, and she would perhaps shoot me in the back if she had a gun. I prepared for the worse, getting ready to turn around to face her. I was carrying a woman in my arms that she despised because of a confession about how she'd felt about me. It was ironic because Gina was the first person drooling over Britt's sex appeal. No doubt she wanted a threesome with her, but I figured that all changed five hours ago. I sighed with a deep breath of relief. Gina was adjusting in small increments, placing the covers over her body. The important thing was that she remained asleep. She'd been up with me through the night waiting for Silva to return. She needed rest as much as I did, if not more.

I looked down at Britt, and she pinned those hazel eyes on me. Something told me to put her down, and she was ok to walk on her own. But I didn't as if I cared enough to protect her from Gina. Even though my ribs were killing me, I didn't. Even though I loved Gina, I didn't. Something was wrong with me. Why did I risk what I had with Gina for Britt? A woman I didn't give a damn about? Maybe it was because of what I did to Kim, was I trying to repent for my sin by trying to protect her?

I got out of there safely and carried Britt to another room that Kane and I used to occupy when we would visit as kids. I laid her down on the bed, gracefully. "You'll need something for that bruise on your jaw. I'll be right back." I turned for the door and felt a restrain on my wrist. Britt's tiny hand barely had any strength. I could have pulled her off of the bed if I wasn't paying attention.

"Thank you," Britt smiled up at me. She looked tired, seconds away from falling asleep.

"Don't thank me," I said, turning away. "I want you to know something. You got me all wrong. I'm not a nice guy. I've done things that I'm not proud of, things that would terrify you. I'm a killer with one goal in mind, and nothing will distract me from being successful. I don't care how beautiful you are and how your feelings are affected. My intention will remain the same. Gina and I are one. You couldn't begin to comprehend how to be by my side. Don't take my kindness for weakness. I wouldn't hesitate to let Gina kill you if it came down to it. Hopefully, I've made myself clear." I left her with that and exited the room.

Chapter 25: Jordan

I pressed send on my phone. It rang twice, and then I hung up. That was part of the process when reaching this particular individual. I got a callback 2 minutes later and answered. "There is a hooker that I need you to look after for a while. I'll send over the details. Same pay as the last job, capeesh." I hung up the phone because the individual on the other line never speaks. All he did was listen, and when the job was done, I'd send payment through a wire transfer. I messaged the details about the whore to the contractor and slipped the phone into my pocket. It was essential for Rick to hear me speak. His little love interest was in danger if he didn't abide by our regulations.

I looked at Rick and smiled, "I wish you could say something. But the look on your face is enough." I walked over to him. "The man I sent after your whore is a trained killer. It doesn't matter to him who's in charge as long as he gets paid. That's his only concern. He won't hesitate to put Cherry in a fruit basket if you know what I mean." I grinned as he looked deep into my eyes. "Oh, and for five hundred, the pussy isn't that great." Rick jumped up and rushed me. He wrapped his arms around my waist, trying for a spear wrestling move. A swift knee to the gut stopped him in his tracks. He doubled over, panting with his head down. I pulled out my gun and pressed it against the top of his head. "I can't believe how you're behaving, rook. You fell in love with a whore. I should kill your soft ass."

"Don't," Adrian said with his hand over the barrel of the gun. "remember the plan."

I smirked. "I was only joking with this asshole. I would never stick my dick in that dirty whore." I sighed and held back the urge to headshot Rick. He straightened up and poked out his chest, trying to appear manly. Water rimmed around his eyes. What I said affected him emotionally. A hooker meant that much to him. "You wouldn't survive that long as an FBI agent feeling that way about a street hooker, my friend." Rick stood there face to face with me. His chest heaving in and out like an angry gorilla. "Rookie," I slapped Rick's head with the butt of my gun.

Rick fell to the floor. The impact was loud enough to shock Mrs. Simmons, and she put her hand over her mouth. She didn't look scared but concerned. I glanced at her while standing over Rick like a champion fighter. "Don't look so concerned about this white boy. He'll be fine." Her eyes went from me to the floor at Rick.

Adrian shook his head at me. "What," I shrugged back at him. "at least I didn't blow his brains out."

"The problem is you're making things worse for us," Ardian said.

"How?" I asked.

127

"His vehicle is close by, and we need to find it," he said. "It would be wise if we used a police vehicle to enter a police impound. Our plans will be delayed until he's up again."

Adrian was half right. Rick's vehicle would be easier to move around in since it's a police cruiser. But he was wrong about our plans being delayed. "It's better to make our move around eight at night. The security is light, and there will be a shift change. We'll hit them then. It's only three, so we have some time on our hands. In the meantime, we should go over a plan because we can't ride with him into the impound."

"What do you suggest we do," Adrian asked and crossed his arms.

I thought long and hard about it. I stepped over Rick and sat down next to Mrs. Simmons. "We need to capture one of the women officers and steal Mrs. Simmons a police badge. You never see one officer trying to inspect a confiscated vehicle alone, let alone an aircraft. That's a two-person job for sure. You and I won't fit the bill because we're wanted, so she's our only option."

"Do you think you can handle that," Adrian asked.

Mrs. Simmons' eyes went from Rick to me, and then Adrian before she answered. "I don't have a choice."

"That's not an answered!" I roared. "Dammit, it's not the time to bitch up." My patience with this woman was short. Jordan and

The Planner had enough. One minute she's ill and the next a gangster. And now she's sick again. The bitch has more mood swings than a pregnant dog. I need to correct her ASAP.

There was no way I would roll with this, Mrs. Simmons. I need the gangster I came across at the TMF mansion.

"I need you to fucking act accordingly. This isn't what I signed up for. I told you before I rather take the money back from Kane. Instead, some gangster bitch convinced me to do something absolutely insane. And for some odd reason, my crazy ass accepted, and now I'm working with this dickhead to my right." Adrian knew I was talking about him but didn't respond. "So what is it going to be, Mrs. Simmons? Can you handle going inside a police impound with this sonovabitch on the ground and jack us an airplane?"

Mrs. Simmons kept her eyes on me. I steadied them, trying to figure out what direction she wanted to go. This situation was her doing. She was the one who'd convinced me to play her game. If she didn't want to get her hands dirty, then it'd be settled. I would no doubt kill her if Adrian didn't first. She needs to remember he's the killer, not me. The only reason she's alive was because of the deal she made with him. He would've slit her throat otherwise. "Well,...Mrs. Simmons?"

She had a serious look in her eyes. I saw that gangster return. "You can call me, Noti."

Chapter 26: Rick

My head was throbbing and felt like it was seconds from exploding. Just moving a tiny bit sent a wave of pain through my entire body. I groaned and opened my eyes. What the fuck had happened? It was hard to recall anything. My mind was blank.

I'm on the floor, I thought. *How did I get here, and why is my head feeling like it been hit with a baseball bat?*

Suddenly I heard the answer in the background. It was Jordan's voice, without a doubt. He was rambling about going inside a police impound and jacking a plane. The second part wasn't that clear, but I did hear Mrs. Simmons' name spill out of his mouth in the next sentence. Jordan was questioning her. I thought I'd gotten drunk and collapsed on my apartment floor, having a bad dream. When I saw the sholes of Jordan's shoes from the floor, I knew that wasn't the case. I slowly grabbed my head, not trying to alert him. I twitched from the pain when I touched the spot that was aching. I felt a hint of blood but not enough to worry about a severe head injury.

I spotted a pair of women's shoes. *Mrs. Simmons,* I thought. "You can call me, Noti." I heard her say as if she was reading my thoughts. Noti is Mrs. Simmons' legal first name. I knew that because I saw it on her passport when I completed a profile on her and Jar Simmons, her husband. But why was she telling

Jordan to call her, Noti? Were they a team or som…that's when it hit me. I remembered why I was on the floor. Jordan had struck me over the head with his pistol. She was working with them, Jordan and Adrian. *Fuck*, I thought. As I regained some strength in my legs, I tried to move.

"He's up," It wasn't Jordan's voice. Black Water! "Get him up so we can find out where he parked the car."

Park the car? Damn, that's right. I came here alone.

Adrian must have expected my vehicle to be somewhere close by. Maybe they looked for the car and couldn't find it while I was out. I groaned as I was hoisted off the floor by my underarms on both sides. Adrian and Jordan worked hand in hand and then placed me on the couch next to Mrs. Simmons.

"Listen, big boy," Jordan was the first to speak. "we need to know where you parked your car?"

My eyes were blurry, and Jordan's ugly snarl slowly came into focus. I didn't respond.

"Can he talk?" Jordan's eyes glanced to the left when he asked the question.

"He should be able to speak," It was Adrian's voice I heard. "the tea shoulda helped by now."

Jordan turned back to me. He stood hunched over in my face. "Alright, motherfucker. I know you can speak, so answer me when I'm talking to you." He slapped my face hard enough

131

to snap my head to the side. "If you don't want Cherry's sweet pink pussy to get ripped open by my friend. I advise you to answer."

I shook off the pain and faced him. I should have spat in his face, but he woulda killed me. That's how much of a manic Jordan had become. Knowing himself was probably difficult for him. I learned about guys who went undercover for as long as Jordan did. They tend to develop a split personality, not able to identify who they really are. Some stay home, and the others became,...well, Jordan. Some army veterans go through the same effect after service, not knowing where to go from there in life.

"It's about a mile out," I told him. "I parked it on the side of the road."

"We have to get to that car fast before someone spots it," Adrian said. "the police could be looking for it by now if he doesn't report."

"Fuck," Jordan said. "it's been a few hours. We need to take Rick with us so he can report to dispatching immediately." Jordan looked at Mrs. Simmons and tossed her a key. "Start the car while we get this pig together."

I had two options. I could pretend to be injured and let them haul me off, or I could move on my own. Both options weren't bad. Playing hurt would only delay their plans because dispatch

132

wouldn't be looking for me. I didn't report what I was doing here in the first place. I'm off duty and wouldn't have to be at the department until sometime tomorrow. I had initially taken the day off to be with Cherry. I guess letting them believe I reported was best.

We left the cabin, and I let them haul me off into the black Cadillac. Jordan complained the entire time while Adrian stayed silent. I could tell he didn't want to be involved with Jordan. They were two different men. I would've never guessed they were brothers. Jordan told Mrs. Simmons to drive while they sat shoulder to shoulder with me in the back. On the way, Jordan decided to get on Mrs. Simmons about her driving skills.

"Can you drive any slower," Jordan complained. "at this rate, we won't get there until tomorrow."

Mrs. Simmons looked through the rearview mirror at Jordan. "I don't drive much, and if all you're going to do is complain. You can drive," she stopped the car in the middle of the road. She crossed her arms and made a nasty facial expression at him.

Multiple vehicles blew their horn as they passed by us. There weren't many vehicles out but enough to cause some uneasiness. A car came speeding down the road in the opposite direction. The vehicle was heading straight at us. Mrs. Simmons had her eyes closed, lip poked out, and her nose turned up while showing the least amount of concern about colliding with another vehicle.

"What the fuck!" Jordan exploded. "Are you fucking crazy!" he grabbed the shoulder of the driver's side seat and yelled in Mrs. Simmons' ear.

"You need to apologize, or we'll sit right here," She said, not giving a damn if the car coming at us would end our lives.

Adrian looked as if he was ready to die. He didn't say a word, and he held a smirk on his face as if this was an exciting game of chicken.

I didn't say anything. If we were going to die, then so be it. At least Jordan would go down with us.

Jordan began to panic, and I guess The Planner wasn't so tough either because they both folded under pressure. "Fuck, I'm sorry!"

Mrs. Simmons smiled and put her hands on the steering wheel and pull off, dodging the oncoming car in the nick of time.

I spotted the person in the car as it shot by. It was a teenage girl paying more attention to her cell phone than the road. I wondered if she even knew she was seconds away from losing her life over a text message that could wait.

"Goddammit," Jordan was out of breath. His chest was moving up and down rapidly. He pounded on the back of Mrs. Simmons' seat out of frustration. I forgot how on edge he could be when his anxiety kicked in. I recalled a few times when I'd brought him coffee back at the office, and he lost his shit. I used to think he was messing around and acting scared when I approached from behind while he worked. But little did I know he'd developed a sense of urgency when he was undercover. An urgency that made him react in a way that said, you're about to die.

We got to my car, and Jordan was the first to get out. He hurried to the driver's side door and erupted at Mrs. Simmons. She stayed inside the vehicle while Jordan bitched at her. Adrian shook his head and got out. He guided me to the side of my car and ordered me to open it. I punched the code in the door, and the locks popped. He put me in the back seat after retrieving the car keys. He locked me inside, knowing I couldn't get out without climbing into the front seat. I couldn't drive off anyway without the key. He searched the front of the vehicle quickly. He found my wallet and the vehicle document in the glovebox. That was all I had besides my cell that I hid under the front seat. Surprisingly, he didn't run a thorough enough check to find it. I could hear Jordan and Mrs. Simmons screaming back and forth at each other. Adrian sighed and went off before things got too heated.

I didn't want to turn around and see what was shaping up from behind. I watched through the rearview mirror. Adrian was smart. He'd backed away from the car with his eyes locked on me, paying close attention to my every move. When he reached Jordan, it created a thirty-second window that gave me a chance to spring into action. I grabbed the phone, went to recent calls, and pressed send. It wasn't the department. *Dammit.* Instead, I'd pressed send on Kane's number by mistake. I didn't have time to correct the problem, so I alerted him of the situation.

Chapter 27: Kane

"Slowdown, Rick," I said. "I can barely understand you."

"I don't have time," Rick said sternly. "so pay attention. Jordan and his brother captured me, and your mother is here. They're taking us to a police impound to hijack an airplane. They're planning to fly to Africa. Contact the FBI and let them know, and a woman named Samantha Higgins is in danger. She's staying at the hotel on 17th street. If things go wrong...don't come looking for your mother."

"Rick-" The line ended. I was speaking to a dial tone. "Shit," I muttered. I looked at the phone while thinking about what Rick said to me a second ago. My main focus was when he mentioned my mother. But, there was something else that caught my attention. Rick had said, Jordan and his brother captured me. I couldn't believe another psychopath was working with The Planner, and it was his brother. Several thoughts came to mind about the evil brothers. Were they both working together the entire time? Had his brother been behind the museum job? Honestly, it didn't matter. I have two lunatics to deal with as opposed to one. *And who the hell is Samantha Higgins?*

"Kane," Smoke snapped me back to reality. "you good, my guy?"

I looked in his direction and saw a concerned look on his face. I felt everyone's attention on me, so before I answered him. I'd glanced around the room. Bear and Big Bruce's eyes were on me. They weren't the only people intrigued about the conversation I just had. My eyes journeyed up the stairs, and I spotted Kim leaning over the balcony, looking down at me. At which point, I wanted to ask how her head felt, but it appeared she was thinking the same as the rest of the crew.

I drew my attention back to Smoke. "The Planner has Rick and my mother." I didn't think about it until now. I'd let Big Bruce hear important information about my family. "He mentioned something about hijacking an airplane so they could fly to Africa."

"I knew it," Bear spoke up.

"What are you talking about?" Kim asked from the balcony.

"Bear had a dream that we were searching for Abel in Africa," I answered for him.

"Do you think Abel's in Africa," Smoke crossed his arms and looked off to the side, contemplating the situation. "and what does that have to do with Rick and mom? Abel working with The Planner or something? Did Rick say anything else?"

"I'm not sure who's in Africa," I said, frustrated, thinking about my mother's situation and the things she'd probably gone through. "All signs have been pointing there. To answer your other question, I don't think Abel and The Planner are working together. That would be insane, but not hard to believe. Rick confirmed that Jordan was working with his brother. Abel wasn't the name he mentioned...he wants me to let the FBI know a woman named Samantha Higgins is in danger."

"The Planner," Big Bruce said. "sounds like a maniac in a thriller."

"That's exactly who he is," Kim had a grim tone in her voice. "your worst nightmare, and now there's two."

The look on Bruce's face told me that he'd believed her.

"Another crazy brother is all we needed," Smoke said sarcastically, shaking his head. "Ok, so maybe it wasn't Abel we were looking for in Bear's dream. It could've been Jordan and his brother. With that being said, why Africa? He doesn't have the diamond. Abel..."

"The black market," I interrupted. It didn't take any time to figure out what was going on. The black notebook came to mind—my father's dark secret and all of the things he'd done and what I learned. I finally realized Abel and The Planner's purpose.

"That's tough," Smoke sighed out of frustration.

"What is that suppose to mean?" Kim asked and came downstairs. She stood between Smoke and me.

"It means whoever wants the diamond is in Africa."

I couldn't believe what I heard come out of Big Bruce's mouth. How the hell did he know about the diamond? I shot a look at Bear, and so did everyone else. He was the only one left with Bruce who could've said something about the diamond. Kim was upstairs, sleeping. And Smoke left the house with me.

Bear looked back at me with an innocent face and shrugged, confirming he didn't inform Bruce of the diamond. What came next took us all by surprise.

"Stop looking at Bear funny," Big Bruce said. "I'm not a stupid guy. I saw it on the news when I was on lockdown. A guard pulled it up on TV after it happened. Breaking news," he smirked. "African war breaks out with FBI agent Jordan. I didn't think about the name until you mentioned him—the same guy who brought you into the detention center. I remember them interviewing a white cop with the same name you also brought up, Rick. The whole thing was over a stolen diamond, and that wasn't what caught my interest. What did was when the white cop said Kane Simmons was under Jordan's influence. I put two and two together, that's all."

"Nigga, you're an informant," Smoke replied. "you got all that info from watching the news? Hell, nah. Kane, I told you he's suspect." Smoke grabbed his strap off the table.

"He's telling the truth," I said. "I watched the same segment."

"Seriously," Smoke retorted. "you think he figured that out by watching one segment? I think somebody fed him information. Maybe they're on to us and sent him." he looked at Bruce. "You just got out, right?"

"When you're locked up," Bruce said. "You make it your business to know about the people you interact with. You'll learn that once you're a big boy."

"Stop," I held my hand out to stop Smoke from making a stupid move on Big Bruce. Another body to clean up wasn't ideal. "Think about what he'd said, Africa. Rick specifically stated, don't come looking for my mother if things go wrong. That's odd because Smoke's right about the diamond, and The Planner hasn't contacted me about it. It leads me to believe their trip has something to do with my father's organization, and they need her. Jordan found out my father was a smuggler. He knew from the beginning. My father's notebook had locations. I remember seeing most of his drop-offs in Libya." I looked at Smoke, concerned.

Kim spoke up. "This isn't about the diamond," Kim spoke up. "They're after your father's money."

Chapter 28: Kim

The day I learned about the notebook, Kane and I were lying in bed, talking about everything that happened while I was in a coma. It was a long night. So many things had happened to him. It's a blessing he got through it alive and with all that money. He told me everything about The Planner's hitman, Ke'Mo Cutt, and how Abel's psycho girlfriend attempted to blow up the hospital room where I was receiving treatment. The General and the death of our friend, Redd. What surprised me the most was the story about the black notebook that belonged to his father.

"His father's money?" Smoke said. "That's ridiculous. What bank would unload that much money?"

"Bank," I replied sarcastically. "You're not looking at the big picture."

"Wait a minute," Bear interrupted. "is it straight to be talking about all this in front of..." he secretly tried to nod his head in Big Bruce's direction.

"Bear," Kane said. "he can see you, big dawg."

"He's fine," I said. "I trust him."

"One minute he's an informant, and the next he's cool," Bear muttered. "Wud da hell."

"You good, right?" Smoke padded the front of his shirt.

Big Bruce didn't respond and sucked his teeth.

"Smoke," I turned to him. "I told you he's good already."

"I got you, sis." Smoke backed off. "Alright, what about the money?"

"What I was trying to say," I sighed, looking at everyone in the room. "The money isn't in a bank. Jordan knew about the smuggling business, and he's not dumb enough to kidnap and haul Mrs. Simmons all the way to Africa without a certified reason. I think Kane is onto something deeper than something unimaginable. What if..." I paused to get the words right. "your father's operation was in Libya, and your mother told him about it?"

"Why would she say something about it to him?" Kane answered with a question.

"Perhaps," I began. "To save her life or yours. Who knows, she probably saved it as a last resort for a bargaining chip."

"Makes sense," Bruce added.

Smoke looked at Bruce like, who the fuck asked you. I eyed Smoke, sighing for him not to say a word, and he listened, surprisingly.

"I could be crazy, but you know how I like to put things together," I said to Kane. "your father had a ton of movement in Lybia from what you'd told me. If that estimate of what you gave me of his worth is true or remotely close, he would need somewhere to stash an overflow of products and cash."

"Like a safe house," Bear looked at me, unsure if he was right, and before I could answer, he muttered. "I mean, that's where I'd put my shit."

"You're right," I said, and his spirit rose again. "but a better word would be…headquarters."

"Like that?" Smoke said, shocked. "Pops was serious."

"A headquarters," Kane muttered. "We can't them take her to Africa. I'll never see her again. The Planner will kill her after he gets what he wants."

"So what do we do?" Smoke throughout there for anyone who could come up with an answer.

"Samantha Higgins," I looked around the room. "Rick said she was in danger, right? Why? How is she involved in all this? We need to find her."

"That won't be a problem," I said. "she's staying in a hotel off 17th street. That shouldn't be hard to find since there are only two hotels by the new restaurant."

"Then let's get something to eat." Smoke tucked his weapon, heading for the door.

"I'm coming too," There was about to be a problem, and I knew it. I turned for the door, and as on cue, Kane grabbed my arm.

"No way," he said to me. "It's too dangerous."

"But-" I started.

"No ifs, ands, or buts about it," he said. "I'm serious. You could get hurt, and you've been through enough already. I need to know you're safe if something pops off."

"Alright," I easily gave in. My plan wasn't to go with him. What I wanted was to keep Bruce and Kane together. That's why I didn't mind sharing the information earlier when I'd said to Bear, he's fine. If Bruce isn't with him, how could he protect him? Although, I need to be careful with my decisions. Bruce is smarter than he first appeared to be. He could have other motives, waiting for the perfect time to get at Kane. Smoke could be right. What if Bruce is an informant? I don't trust him one bit, but in the end. He's another shield of armor for my soldier. "Take Bruce with you."

Kane looked at me, ready to retort.

I silenced him before the words could come out of his mouth. "No ifs, ands, or buts about it."

Chapter 29: Abel

I closed the door after giving Britt two ibuprofens and a glass of water. I walked back to my room and stopped at the door to peep inside. Gina was sound asleep and facing the doorway. I thought about resting for another hour or two; my body could use it. I went back downstairs to the living room. Snake had his phone in his hand. His fingers were moving rapidly, tapping the screen one at a time. Bam sat on the couch in front of the TV, watching World News.

I sat down on the sofa chair next to a side table with a lamp on it. I picked up the black notebook to go over shipments in Africa. Anything to get my mind of the pain in my chest. It wasn't as bad as before, but it was still irritating. In a couple more hours, I could see some kind of doctor. My eyes went from the book to Bam. He had a huge smile on his face. "What's funny?"

"You know," Bam adjusted his body, turning it in my direction. "the woman Britt. Gina doesn't like her, and you do."

I didn't respond immediately to his accusation when I should have. Gina could have said something while I was upstairs. Of course, Bam would want this to be the case. "Don't get side-tracked. You're smarter than that, my friend."

"I'm just making small talk," Bam said. "It's better than sitting around here doing nothing. I'm not the only one who wants to know." His eyes signed at Snake.

Snake was focused on his phone and appeared not to be paying attention to our conversation. "Is that true, Snake?"

"It would be nice to have something else going on for a change." Snake said. "We left college where we worked our asses off. All we have been doing since coming to town is work. Life or death situations, I'd like to add. I didn't have any experiences with women during my time there, and neither did Bam. You get to interact with Gina."

I know what the boys were hinting at, and they wanted a chance with Britt without me interfering. I could understand where they were coming from. Neither man had an opportunity with a woman since being in town. They had worked their asses off, and what did they get for it? A few bullets sent their way and a knockout punch from a gorilla. I sent for them to help with something more important than any of our desires. In between that, it wouldn't hurt to have some fun. "She's not off-limits. I don't like her at all. You two have at her."

"Are you serious," Snake asked. "because you guys were in the room long enough to get to know each other well."

I smiled. "Would it make a difference if I told you nothing happened?"

"Not really," Bam said. "she's smoking hot. I hope she likes me."

"You don't have a chance in hell," Snake eyed Bam. "She'll be on my side like Gina is with Abel."

"Whoever is the better man," I said seriously to them both. "Keep her out of Gina's way. I don't want Britt messing with Gina's head. That could be bad for all of us."

"Why would you say that," Snake asked. "They looked friendly with each other two hours ago."

"When you have beautiful women around men of our stature," I began. "you have to be cautious about their feelings. Let this be a lesson. Most women of their caliber want money or power. That's it. But there are a few who fall in love with a man's mind, Britt is one of them, and Gina is all three."

"What does that suppose to mean?" Bam asked with a confused look on his face.

"She's a sapiosexual," I told them. "and I'm more intelligent than both of you."

"Ha," Snake laughed. "Funny, I remember kicking your ass in chess last game."

I smiled. I tried to show a different side than the regular brand of humor I possess. Britt and Gina's confrontation, I kept to myself. I rather have them think they have a chance with her to keep their spirits up. I know what a team plays like when they're not having fun. We could get focus on the goal once we're in Africa.

Snake sat his phone to the side and sighed. "How about her husband? Is he a killer?"

I can hold my own against any man. Bam and Snake are more on the intelligence over brawn side of the field. And we know what Kane's friend did to Snake. They're attracted to Britt but fighting an overconfident man in the ring won't be an option. That fight would never happen. Geniuses stick to being geniuses, and fighters stick to being fighters. When is the last time a nerd became a world champion in the cage? "She isn't married."

"Wha," Snake's face lit up. "she isn't married?"

"I thought you said she was," Bam asked.

"Did you see a ring on her finger?" I watched both of their facial expressions. They seem to be in thought if there were a ring on Britt's finger. "Alright then, enough about her." I sat the notebook back on the table. There was nothing new I could learn from it. My plan was simple. Get the diamond to the General and secure my father's warehouse. From there, the safe should be easy enough to find. "We are hours away from being in front of fear. The part of Africa that we're traveling to is very dangerous. We need to prepare ourselves from the beginning. The General won't hesitate to put a bullet in our heads or get one of his low-life soldiers to do it." I stood from the chair. It was better to explain the plan to them while Britt wasn't

149

around. I didn't want her nose in our business. Gina was well aware of my plan. I got a chance to have an extended conversation with her in my parent's bed before the rib injury.

"This is what we're going to do. Snake, I need you to look up the gear the rebels are wearing and purchase matching attire for me. I'm the only man of size that could possibly get by as one of them. You two, along with Gina, will blend in with the community. Who knows how long we'll be there and we don't need any problems with anyone. The General will be challenging to get in front of with the insane amount of men I would have to bribe." I turned my attention on Bam. "We'll need supplies, anything useful to survive while we're there. That includes food and water. Gina will be in charge of guarding the fort. The diamond has to be kept safe at all costs. Without it, we have nothing. We need to move accordingly for the entire time until I can reach the General and make the deal for the headquarters."

"What if we make this trip and still come up empty-handed?" Bam asked. "How can you be sure the General knows where your father's headquarters is located?"

"The army controls the land," I told him. "At the level Jar was operating at as a high-value smuggler, it would've been in the General's best interest to know a man of that much importance with that amount of artillery influence. He's not a visitor on your land making money. He's a partner."

"Milk the man," Snake muttered. "not the land."

"And Bam," I had to check him about the ignorance that spilled from his mouth. "don't ever call Jar my father again, or I'll kill you."

Chapter 30: Kane

We piled in the Humvee, riding suspect. Smoke sat in the passenger's seat while Bear and Big Bruce rode in the back of the truck. We looked like four black men in a black truck, looking for trouble...and that was exactly what we were doing on 17th street. I had to give it up to Kim for playing a part in this unusual predicament. She suggested bringing Big Bruce.

How did I let her convince me to bring him?

What we were going to do was dangerous. Bruce could fold under pressure if something went sideways. How would he act in an unpredictable situation? I glimpsed at Bruce through the review mirror unnoticeably and then put my eyes back on the road. He was looking out of the window and more than likely felt my eyes on him. The fact that he knew about the diamond and my history with Jordan didn't taste good. T-Mac let him get close, but it wouldn't be that easy with me. The saying of keeping your enemies close was in full effect. My enemy sat in the backseat behind me.

"Pull over right here," Smoke pointed at a parking spot in front of the corner store. "There's one of the hotels. We don't want anyone to spot us pulling up to the joint. Some shit could go down."

"We don't wanna look like four football players walking into a hotel either," Bruce spoke up.

"Yeah," Bear said, looking over at the hotel from between the seats. "that wouldn't be cool."

Both of them were thinking smart. "Only two of us will go inside. Bruce, your face is banged up, so you'll wait in the truck. Bear, you were good at keeping this guy company, so you'll stay with him. Drive the whip around the block a few times, slowly."

Bear spoke up while I was reaching for my phone. "If we only knew what she looks like, that would've been helpful."

I found what I was looking for in a text message. "I got you. This is a picture of Samatha Higgins." I showed each of them the photo."

"White girl," Bear said. "with red hair. She shouldn't be too hard to find."

"How did you get that?" Smoke asked. "and you sure that's her?"

"My guy," I looked at Smoke. "you think that I wouldn't be sure about something like this?"

"My bad," Smoke said. "you do be on your Sherlock Holmes shit."

"True dat," Bear added.

"After you guys left the house," I explained. "I called Tang after I finished talking with Kim. I asked if he and could find anything on Samatha. He's the real deal, Smoke, you know that. I got this text from him right before I got in the truck."

"Damn," Bruce said. "that fast?"

"That fast," I replied. "He's that smart. This has to be Samatha. Smoke and I will go inside to look for her. If things get hot, we'll call and go from there. Same if you spot her. Bear, I'll send the photo to your phone." I forward the photo to Bear's phone while getting out of the vehicle. Smoke got out, and I met him on the passenger's side of the Humvee. Bear hopped in the driver's seat, and Bruce moved to the front. He let down the window on our side. "Alright, be safe out there. Remember, any problems hit my line." I nodded and began walking to the first hotel with Smoke.

I didn't look at the truck as it passed by us. I kept it moving, focused on finding Samatha. The picture was a good idea. It's incredible how Tang was able to come through for me that quick. Smoke matched my steps. We were moving at the same pace. He had a calm look on his face, and I thought he would appear more serious. Ever since Bruce showed up at my doorstep, Smoke had been with me, and I didn't think he'd go home if he knew Bruce was around. That was out of the question.

A few people were walking around the area, not many. Some were sitting outside of the restaurant, dining. I watched two men walk inside a bike store. A group of women all dressed up in church clothes walked in our direction. They all looked to

154

be in their fifties. I got a feeling they would approach us and ask questions about the word, trying to preach the good gospel. There's nothing wrong with that, but time was running short.

"Excuse us, young man," one of the ladies spoke up. She was wearing a sun straw hat with a bowknot, blue dress, and grandma heels. "I would like a moment to tell you about our Lord and Savior, Jesus-"

"I'm sorry, but the Lord hasn't been good to me lately," I interrupted before she could get started preaching our ears off.

"The Lord is good to everyone," The lady countered. "You have to keep praying and-"

The woman kept going on and on about how I should get down on my knees and pray every day. She began to dive into bible scriptures and how to live a righteous life. I let out a noticeable sigh and looked at Smoke. He appeared fed up with listening to the lady preach. He met my stare, and it was a mutual sign of agreement to end this conversation.

"And you have to ask the Lord for forgiveness," she continued. "can I get a hallelujah!"

"Hallelujah, Amen," each of the women responded simultaneously. One of the women began fanning the woman who was preaching as if she was in an intense battle with the sun.

"Thank you, and I'm sorry," I said. "but we have to go."

"Oh, the Lord," she said. "is patient with you, so you have to be patient with the Lord! Can I get a hallel-"

"Dammit," Smoke erupted. "hallelujah! Now that's enough. We have to get the hell out of here. My friend's mother was kidnaped, and the only way to get her back is to find a redhead named Samatha. If the Lord can't help us with that, get the hell outta the way because we're about to involve ourselves in some gangsta shit."

Oh man, Smoke snapped on the preaching woman. She had a puzzled facial expression for a few seconds before smiling. It was like the Lord entered her body and told her to keep good faith. The other women covered their mouths and started to mumble amongst themselves. I thought they were about to give Smoke a lesson on respect, but that wasn't the case.

The preaching woman looked at Smoke with a glare in her eyes. "What do your young ass know about gangsta shit? I've been working these streets my entire life, doing drugs, stealing, popping my pussy, anything for money." She snapped her neck while speaking.

"Hallelujah," they all chanted. "you tell him, sista."

"The Lord," she continued. "told me not to whoop your ass for disrespecting us like that. Instead, he wants me to help resolve your problem."

"Hallelujah, sista," one said. "we have to help these demons and bring them back to our side."

I looked at Smoke like, what the hell just happened? He had the same confound look as I did. We both were lost by how the women transformed from holy to savage. "Did she say, popping my pussy?" I whispered out of the side of my mouth.

"Damn right I did," she answered. "The Lord knows and forgives."

"Hallelujah," they chanted. "Amen."

"Child," the woman emphasized. "Tell us how we can help?"

Something inside of me said this woman could help. I wasn't sure if the Lord spoke to me or just pure instincts—when you get to a response point and don't react when you're supposed to. I pulled out my cell and showed them the picture of Samatha. "We're looking for this woman. She might have some information that could help find my mother."

"Cherry," one of the women said in a low tone.

"Praise the Lord," the preaching woman spoke. "But that whore can't be saved. She's been around the block enough times to need a new set of feet."

"I was told her name was Samatha Higgins," I said. "The Lord may have confused you."

"No child," the woman said with confidence. "that's Cherry. I know a hoe when I see a hoe. You can't hide from the Lord."

157

"It ain't worth five hundred, I can tell you that much." One spoke in an angry tone.

"If we had got paid that much back in the day," another said. "Oh, Lord, help me, Jesus." She whipped sweat from her forehead. "We'd be rich."

"Don't you start, Annamay," the leader of the group said. "We made enough. The salary cap went up after the Lord saved us. We don't play that game, no mo."

"Hold up," Smoke held his hand out. "she's a prostitute?"

"Prostitute ain't the word, child," the woman said. "she's a demon. I tried over and over again to save her, but the devil has a stronghold on that box."

"Do you know where we can find her," I asked?

"I can," she looked in the direction of the hotel. "she does the devil's work in that place. Be careful around her, or you'll be five hundred dollars short. Can I get a hallelujah!"

"Hallelujah, sista," they chanted. "Amen."

"She's on the third floor," another said.

"And how do you know that, sista," the leader snapped her neck.

"The deacon and I used a room earlier for bible study," she said.

"Um-hum.." the leader rolled her eyes. "y'all could've used the church."

"Well," I said. "We enjoyed our time with you, and thank you for your help. We have to get going now." I turned to Smoke. "Let's bounce."

We smiled at the women and walked off toward the hotel. I heard the women getting on the one who was with the deacon. I was glad they were because it kept them from holding us up. We made it to the front of the hotel. I pinned my dreads back, trying not to look aggressive. I know how people in high-end establishments acted toward men who look like thugs. We weren't dressed in suits, so you know how it gets. And to make matters worse, we were looking for a prostitute.

Chapter 31: Jordan

"If you ever want to see your son again," I looked at Mrs. Simmons through the driver's side window. She closed her eyes and crossed her arms over her chest. "Stop pretending that you don't hear me. I will fucking murder you and Kane if you ever put my life in danger again. That was your final warning."

Adrian walked up and grabbed my shoulder. "This needs to-"

I slapped his arm away, angry at what happened earlier in the car. "Get your fucking hand off me." I walked away, heading for Rick's vehicle. "I'm done." My hands were both up, signing I wasn't a threat. I heard Adrian say something, but I didn't catch what he said. I had tuned him out. Listening to anything else he had to say could have been my breaking point.

I got to Rick's car and opened the front door. He sat in the backseat, looking like a crook. The vehicle was off, and I didn't see a key in the ignition. The damn thing wasn't anywhere in sight. I sat up straight, head faced toward the road. "he has the key."

"That would be a yes, compadre," Rick answered from the backseat.

We locked eyes through the rearview mirror. "It wasn't a question," the words came out harsh. *Fuck,* I thought. I have to get out of the car and ask Adrian for the key. That got me even more frustrated, and I felt like letting off a couple of rounds in the air. It got quiet when I got out of the car. I could hear the gravel under my tennis shoes as I walked back to Adrian. We still got a few hours before going to the police impound, and I already had enough bullshit for the day.

I stopped two feet away from Adrian and held out my hand. Mrs. Simmons hadn't moved from the driver's seat. I kept a straight face without looking in her direction, avoiding her the satisfaction of knowing how I felt. Adrian had the same look on his face, matching my appearance. "I know you're not stupid enough to leave the key with him. Give it to me? You'll be with her. We'll take both vehicles."

Adrian held the key up in the air in front of my face. "Don't get comfortable." He let the key go, and it dropped in my palm. "I'm hungry."

I caught the key as it landed in my hand. Adrian walked past and around the car. "We shouldn't be in public." I stood there looking aimlessly at the ground.

"It's a bar down the road," I heard him open the car door. "I ate there before, good food."

I sighed and looked up. I was standing alone. That meant I didn't have an option. If Adrian ate at the bar, then it's a safe location. He wouldn't put his life in jeopardy over some good food. I put my pride to the side and walked back to the car.

161

Rick spoke up when I got inside. "So I'm stuck with you." He snarled.

I adjusted the seat to match my size. My legs needed more room. *Short guys,* I thought. Rick wanted to get under my skin, and I could have responded to him. Jordan had to be in control for me to get through this–Mrs. Simmons, Rick, and Adrian could get overwhelming, and it would cause me to explode. I remembered what my goal was—my reason for being in this situation in the first place.

Money, I thought—*the good oh American dollar.*

I put the key in the ignition and started the car. It cranked right up without a problem. The sound of a good engine soothed me every time. There was something about it that made me feel calm.

Adrian and Mrs. Simmons drove by us in the car. I pulled out behind them and tailed the vehicle close enough to kiss the bumper. The coast was clear. There were no other drivers on the road at the time. They began to pull away. I pressed the gas pedal down a tad to keep up with them. The Cadilac's motor could easily outperform the V-12 in Rick's police cruiser. Mrs. Simmons had pissed me off, and I felt like getting on her damn nerves. You could call me petty, but fucking with the mind of other people is what I do, and I love it.

After ten seconds, the Cadilac began to gain some separation. Someone finally realized I was acting like an asshole. I smiled and applied more pressure on the gas pedal. I got close enough to the car to ride the bumper for ten more seconds. If Mrs. Simmons had decided to slam on the breaks, there would have been a bad accident. The needle on the tachometer jumped to a high rpm. Both vehicles were moving at an alarming pace at a close distance.

She wanna put my life in danger, I thought.

"You're playing a dangerous game," Rick said from over the seat.

I sucked my teeth and eyed him through the rearview mirror. "Shut up, nobody asked you." My eyes focused back on the road ahead.

"You're a bigger idiot than I thought," I heard Rick laugh. "You left those two alone. What if they come up with a plan to cut you out of the deal?"

I'd thought about that accruing beforehand. I prepared myself for the worse outcome when it's all said and done. That's a lesson I learned from top mafia guys. DTA, don't trust anybody. Wait…I learned that from Stone Cold Steve Austin. My mistake, but same concept. "It'll be me they'll have to worry about in the end." I glanced at him through the rearview mirror. The expression on his face said he expected me to say

163

something to that degree. He didn't respond, and I watched him sit back in the seat. He suddenly appeared nervous, and his movements were suspect. I know when someone is hiding something from me. Rick definitely had something up his sleeve. He's not the type to go down in a fight easily. "Stop moving around back there." I couldn't give him all of my attention, so I decelerated the car to prevent an accident. Mrs. Simmons could have it for now. Her time would come. Now that the vehicle was moving at a slower pace, I could focus on Rick. "What the hell are you trying to hide?"

Rick had an apprehensive look on his face. Sweat rolled down his forehead, and he wiped it away nervously. "I haven't had a cup of coffee today. That's all."

Bullshit, I thought. I haven't had a cup of coffee, I mocked. "Don't fuck with me. I know you're up to something, and when I find-" *Fuck!* We sped past a state trooper.

"Oh, boy," Rick comment from the back. "he's coming to get you."

"Fuck," I banged my fist against the steering wheel as the state trooper turned on his sirens and pulled out after us.

Chapter 32: Rick

"Don't forget about your whore," Jordan's eyes stared at me through the rearview mirror. I was nervous because I dropped the cell phone on the floor. Sweat rolled down my face and traveled into my left eye. It began to twitch, making me seem even more suspect. I saw the sirens of the state vehicle through the right side mirror. He wanted us to pull over. I got myself together as Jordan began to stop the car on the side of the road. I had two options. I could sign to the trooper Jordan's a threat or keep Cherry safe until I'm sure Kane delivered my message to the police.

When would I know that? I thought—*the police impound.*

Maybe, but it's a longshot. If agents show, then he was successful. I looked down at the phone and watched it slide under the seat when the car came to a complete stop.

Adrian and Mrs. Simmons continued in the car ahead of us. They drove the car into a bar parking lot I could see further down the road. It was Jordan's fault we're in this situation for playing mind games, driving like a manic while a wanted suspect. That was genius. I took a deep breath as the trooper approached Jordan's side window and knocked on it with the knuckle of his index finger. His brim hat, dark aviator sunglasses, and thick mustache reminded me of a guy in a movie I saw in 2001.

Jordan let down the window, and the officer spoke. "License and registration."

I had to think fast. It would have been easier if I were sitting in the front seat. "We're agents with the FBI, and this is an official police vehicle."

The officer looked at Jordan suspiciously and then turned his attention on me. "Agents, huh," he went back to Jordan. "License and registration."

The trooper kept a straight face behind his aviator glasses. "My wallet is in the glovebox." I nodded toward the compartment.

"What about you," the officer asked Jordan. "are you a special agent too?" He said sarcastically.

The trooper didn't know Jordan was a wanted man. He would've recognized his face by now. Jordan might have had the time to get fake documentation, but it wouldn't work in this case. His face would come back a match as a wanted man. Jordan had to kill the officer to get out of this situation.

"The compartment is empty," Jordan said with an even tone in his voice.

What, I thought. "It was just-" Adrian took it when he had searched the vehicle. That was a smart move to keep my wallet with him for many different reasons.

The trooper's head turned in my direction. I could tell he was upset. His dark glasses shaded the color of his eyes. They were probably on fire. I thought he kind of looked stupid, staring at me without moving for about thirty seconds. I was beginning to think he fell asleep with his eyes on me. Suddenly, he spoke. "License and registration." His head slowly turned in Jordan's direction. It was kind of scary. It was his way of saying, don't say shit else, or you're going to jail.

This situation was about to get ugly. I claimed to be an FBI agent from the backseat of a car without any identification. And I had to convince a state trooper who I was—what a predicament. I wanted to know what Jordan was thinking. I had to keep trying to prove my identity, or this officer was going to die. "My name is Rick Chase. Look up my credentials in the department database."

The trooper sucked his teeth. He didn't give me any attention as he spoke. "Why are you in the backseat, special agent Rick Chase?" He stood straight up and kept his hand on his holster. The strap was unclipped, making it easier to draw the weapon. Typical officer protocol, that wasn't anything to worry about.

"I'm sick," I lied. It was the only idea I could come up with at the time. "Upset stomach, and it's more room back here in case I let loose by accident."

The trooper pulled out a pen and pad. "Rick Chase," he muttered while jotting down my name. "And your name?" he looked at Jordan.

"Sam Collins," Jordan said without any hesitation. "I don't seem to have my identification either. Must have left it at the office."

"Sam..." the trooper jotted down. "Collins," he sighed and looked through the window at us. "Two agents without a way to identify themselves. Well, that's just great. You boys sit tight and keep the vehicle off. I'll be right back."

I read the nametag on the officer's chest before he walked off, *Rabbit.* That's a horrible last name, I thought. Jordan's eyes caught my attention through the rearview. "Sam Collins?"

"It's a fake agent profile I created a long time ago," he said. "No picture, the agent description reads that I'm currently undercover. If it doesn't pass," he adjusted in the seat. I heard click-clack, the loading sound of a gun.

He was going to kill this guy. "You don't have to murder anybody," I looked over at the bar. Mrs. Simmons and Adrian remained in the car. They had yet to move. Adrian was surveying the situation. Would they give themselves up if Jordan murdered this guy? "My credentials should put us in the clear. There's no need to worry. Put the gun away."

"Who said I was worried," Jordan said, turning his head just a bit to peek at the officer through his side mirror.

I peeped out of the other side mirror. The trooper was taking up a lot of time. *What's he doing,* I thought. He found out who Jordan really is. That had to be the case. I didn't see any vehicles on the road. There were no bystanders outside of the bar to see what was going on. And it was foggy in the area. Jordan could murder this guy without anyone ever knowing about it except me. The door of the state vehicle opened, but the officer didn't get out. He was speaking on the dispatch radio and looking at us. That was a bad sign that he had called for backup. Finally, the trooper got out and headed in our direction.

The officer leveled his head with the window, peering through it. Jordan let it down, and I could hear the motor powering it. That's how nervous I was. He didn't say anything, just studied us for a moment. He gave me the impression that he was still unsure about our identity. The officer turned his head in my direction. It seemed to have moved slower than the first time. Again, not a sound. I wondered if the guy even blinked once at us. Those dark shades kept his eyes from revealing how he felt.

What he said next completely took me by surprise. "License and registration?" he kept a straight face while looking at Jordan.

"What…" Jordan sounded confused.

There is no way he just asked the same question again, I thought. I was baffled. "There has to be some kind of mistake. My credentials should have shown on-"

The trooper swiftly backed away from the vehicle and put his hand on his weapon. "I'm gonna need you, gentleman, to step out of the vehicle, please."

Dammit. This officer just pulled the death ticket on his life. There was nothing I could do to save him. Jordan would end him once he stepped out of the car. I had a tough decision to make. I couldn't save this guy without risking everything. I had to come to terms with the fact the trooper was going to die. I heard Jordan's door open. I didn't bother reaching for my door handle. It would be over soon. If anything, I would have to help Jordan dump the guy in the woods somewhere. That would bring on an unpleasant feeling.

Just when Jordan was about to step out. The trooper began to laugh. "I'm just messin' with you guys." He slapped his hand across his knee. "Agents, you're good to go."

What just happened, I thought. This situation was becoming stranger by the minute. Everything that had happened was out of the ordinary. My eyes went from the officer to Jordan. He was standing outside of the vehicle with his hand inside of his jacket.

"The information you gave me was correct," the trooper said. "I felt like getting a laugh out of it since you were in the backseat like an idiot." He kept laughing and continued. "But you, agent Collins. You kind of remind me of someone."

Just get back in the car Jordan, I thought.

The officer didn't pay Jordan's hand any mind. It was on his weapon, no doubt. He had a sinister expression on his face—the face of a demon.

"That's right," the trooper pointed at Jordan. "you look like the man who-"

Vroom...

Out of nowhere, a truck with mud tires and a rebel flag attached to it sped by and nearly struck the trooper.

The trooper maneuvered out of the way in time. He stumbled around and grabbed the top of his hat as he regained his footing. "Holy shitfucker!" he took off running and got inside his vehicle and sped off after the truck.

I sighed and let my head hit the back headrest. *That was close,* I thought. And things were only going to get even more dangerous.

Chapter 33: Kane

Smoke and I stopped a short distance from the hotel. We didn't want to stand in front of the place having a conversation, looking suspect. We had to come up with a plan once we got inside of the building. The churchwoman said she was on the 3rd floor. We had to start there to cut time. "I'll take the elevator, and you got the stairs. That way, we can cover the entrances to the 3rd floor."

"Hold up for a second," Smoke had a puzzled look on his face. "Why do you get to take the elevator?"

"Because you smell like a pound of weed," I said, "You been smoking all day. You don't want anybody looking at you suspiciously. If Samatha does use the stairs, chances are she'll be alone. Which makes for a better conversation on your part."

"I don't know how you do it," Smoke said incredulously, "but I like the way you put things in perspective. Especially when I'm high."

I smiled. Smoke acts funny as hell when he gets high. He didn't even smell like weed, but I knew I could convince him he did. I just wanted him to take the stairs, honestly. "Right," I said with sarcasm. "As I was saying, when we get on the 3rd level, I'll start with the low numbers, and you got the high end. We'll meet in the middle. We'll knock on every door until we find her if that's what it takes."

"Every door," Smoke asked. "I'm cool with that. I heard it's some baddies in this spot."

"Smoke," I emphasized his name with a serious look on my face. "focus."

"I got you," he said. "simple."

I kept my eyes on him as I turned away. "A'ight." We walked to the front of the hotel and looked through the glass front doors before stepping inside. The scene was incredible. There were a bunch of people on the inside doing all sorts of things. "What the…" I muttered. I'd never seen that many people in business suits in one place; then again, I did at my trial.

"This isn't your average hotel," Smoke said. "How in the hell are we supposed to act normal around these people? Shit looks like wall street inside there. The rooms have to be expensive as hell."

"If it's five hunnid to get some ass," I said, reaching for the doorknob. "It's at least a band for a room."

"Bet that," Smoke stepped inside after I opened the door.

I walked in behind him. "I feel like we should of worn suits. I didn't expect it to be like this."

"True dat," Smoke scanned around the front lobby. "found the stairs."

"Bet," I searched for the elevators. "I'm over there. We should look around for a moment. There's a dining area with a bar. Let's check it out first." We walked nonchalantly over to the bar. It was more settled than anywhere else. People were dressed casually but still looked like money. "Two minutes, give or take, and then we'll move on," I said from the side of my mouth.

Smoke kept his eyes on the crowd. "It shouldn't be that hard to spot a redhead."

There was a huge chandelier that caught my attention. It was designed of what I assume to be pure gold and crystals that gave off a rainbow effect.

I heard Smoke say, "I don't see her."

I looked down, just below the chandelier. "My guy," I gently hit Smoke on the chest to get his attention. "There she is," I didn't want to put eyes on us by pointing.

"Where," he looked around.

"Under the chandelier," I said at a low volume. "Standing next to the guy with the funny hair."

"How do you know that's her," Smoke kept his eyes on the woman. "We can't see her face."

"How many redheads with a body like that do you think we're gonna find in this place?" I began walking slowly in the direction of the woman. "We need to get closer."

"Here we go," I heard Smoke mutter from behind.

Smoke held me back by the shoulder.

"Whaddup," I turned around to face him.

"It's not her," he said. "We need to move on."

"Wha," I looked at him, confused. "Did you see her face?"

"Nah," he said, looking past me. "But I can tell by the shape of her ass."

"Nig," I started to call him a word I didn't like to use. "The shape of her ass?" I said sarcastically. "Man, c'mon and let's stop wasting time."

"For real," Smoke said seriously. "We're looking for a prostitute. Not a woman with a well-shaped ass like she'd been working in the gym. Hoe's don't have time to hit the gym like that. They're fuckin' all day." He signaled toward the woman with his eyes. "That woman over there doesn't have a worn-out ass, I'm telling you. I'll hit that fo five hun-don."

I wouldn't know where to begin if we're talking about what a prostitute's ass is supposed to look like. I had never looked at another woman like I did with Kim. I got a general idea of what to look for in a prostitute. Nine times out of ten, she would wear a wig, maybe some high heels, a fancy dress, and give off the appearance of a freak, ready for whatever you want to do with her. That was my impression of one, but Smoke's idea was on another level. Maybe he'd been with one and never mentioned it to me? *Nah,* I shook that thought from my mind.

175

I thought about what Smoke had said, and I came up with a response. "Let's say you're right, but...did you ever consider a prostitute worth five hunnid would possibly look different from a two dolla hoe? What I'm saying is if I were to pay for a high-end hoe, she better be in fantastic shape for that amount of moolah." He looked to be contemplating what I said. "You feel me?"

"A'ight," Smoke agreed. "I didn't think about it that way."

"Cool," I sighed. "We'll move around and get a look at her face before approaching her. If it's not her, we'll continue with the plan." I turned around after I knew everything was straight with Smoke. "No," I muttered. "She's gone."

Smoke stepped in front of me and scanned the area. "Fuck, she must have gotten away when we were talking. My fault."

"Don't trip," I said while searching for Samantha. It happened that quick. I took my eyes off who I believed to be Samatha for ten seconds, and she vanished. I hurried through a crowd of people, even shoving some of them out of the way. It felt like we were attending a party inside a ballroom. Finally, I spotted the woman getting on the elevator. The guy with the funny hair was with her. He blocked me from seeing her face. The elevator doors closed on them.

"Elevator," I pointed out to Smoke.

Smoke beat me to the punch. He stood in front of the elevator, pressing the up button. "Shit takin' too long." He continued to press the button rapidly.

"Stop pressing the damn button," I slapped his hand away. "It stopped on three." I'd watched a light illuminate each floor the elevator was on.

Smoke backed away, "Stairs, we can catch them before they hit the room." He broke for the entrance door, leading the stairway.

I took off behind my best friend. I had a good feeling it was her. It could have turned out worse, but at least I knew she was on the third floor. This whole thing began with my father, I thought. Now I'm chasing after a redhead.

Smoke pushed through the door, and I followed behind him. I jumped up multiple stairs at a time that I'd caught and past Smoke. I reached the third level and opened the door like I had common sense. I inhaled as I stepped over the threshold. I had to catch my breath, and each time I'd landed after a jump, pain entered my side. It was still lingering from the fight with Big Bruce. Thinking about it made me what to punch him in the face.

"Did you see where she went?" Smoke asked, entering the hallway.

"Nah," I replied. The hallway was completely empty on both ends. "I missed them."

"Damn," he muttered. "we're getting slow, bruh."

"You are," I said. "It's the weed."

"I know," he said. "I gotta stop. Shit makin' me lazy."

"I didn't know it was gonna be this many rooms," I looked down the hall. It was a door leading into another hallway. "It's gonna take us forever to find them if we don't get lucky." I could see about 30 rooms just in our section of the floor. I spotted a golden plate with room numbers and directions. "One hundred rooms," I muttered to myself.

"Maybe it won't have to take long," Smoke said.

I looked at him. The expression on his face told me he was on to something. "Got something?"

"Two Spanish women just turned the corner," he said, looking in their direction.

"What about them?"

"They work here," he said. "and if we're lucky, they might know what room she's in."

Smoke didn't wait for an answer. He approached the women like he'd met them before. I caught up to him, and I stood next to a cart. I looked the women over. They had on cleaning uniforms and a pushcart full of work supplies. I assume they were in their forties. Smoke asked them if they'd seen a woman with red hair, and the woman responded in Spanish.

"English, mama," Smoke asked. "Si."

"Si," one replied with a smile. "a little." She had a Spanish accent.

"Did you see a woman with red hair?" Smoke pointed to his dreads.

"Rojo," the woman said. "pelo?"

"What," Smoke said and turned to me. "Do you know what she said? I didn't take Spanish."

I didn't know that much Spanish, but I knew what Rojo meant. "Not his hair, a woman with...a Mamacita with Rojo." I grabbed my hair to show what I was talking about.

The women covered their mouths, and both made a funny face at me.

I felt like asking the women for help was getting nowhere. Then I thought of something I should have done first. I retrieved my phone from my pocket and pulled up the photo of Samatha Higgins. "Have you seen this woman?" I held the phone up to their faces.

I could see in their eyes that the picture of Samatha caught their attention. It didn't take long for them to study the image. The woman who spoke the first time said, "prostituta." She made an unpleasant gesture by pretending to spit on the floor.

Both women began rambling in Spanish at high speed between each other. I noticed something on the cart that I didn't before, and I swiped it before anyone could notice.

I swayed back toward Smoke. I couldn't understand a word the women were saying. One thing I knew for sure, they knew Samatha was a prostitute. Whatever the case may be, we got a lead. "Si, a prostitute. On this floor." I signed by spinning my index finger in a circle.

"Malo," the other woman waved her hand off at me. "chugga chugga."

"Me," I pointed at my chest. "Nada," I played it cool. I thought she saw what I did, but she was referring to having sex with a prostitute.

"Bien," she smiled.

"Room," I said and pointed at a random door.

"Habitacion," she replied to me but looked at the other woman.

The one who was speaking at first spoke up. "Room," she took the lead, heading down the hall.

I thought about what lied ahead as we walked to the room. Smoke had a straight look on his face. He didn't seem to be afraid of anything since his grandmother pass. You could say the same about my father and me. Samatha Higgins could have worked with my father, I thought. She has to know something if she's in danger. I was about to find out. The women stopped in front of room 305 and turned to us. They both looked disgusted.

"Gracias," I said and smiled.

"De nada," they said one at a time. They both put on a fake smile and pushed the cart away.

"Sheesh," Smoke rubbed the back of his neck. "I felt the heat off them."

I watched the women turn the corner. My phone lit up in my hand as I swiped across the screen. I texted Bear and told him we'd found Samantha and the room number.

"You wanna knock?" Smoke asked.

"Nope," I showed him a keycard I'd swiped off the cleaning cart.

Smoke removed his gun from under his shirt. "That's what the fuck I'm talkin' about."

I got my weapon ready. Rick said she was in danger, but she didn't seem to be in trouble in the dining area, standing next to the guy with the funny hair. My father told me to move like you would in chess. Not being armed would be checkmate. My life has been in jeopardy more times in the past year than most people's entire life. Why would death stop coming for me now?

I stuck the keycard in the slot on the door to unlock it. The women had a universal card, as I thought. That's one for the home team. The door key mechanism made a buzzing sound

181

signifying it was open. I looked at Smoke and signed by nodding my head.

He put his ear to the door and shrugged that he didn't hear anything.

I didn't hear anything after focusing my attention on any movement coming from the other side of the door. I figured nobody was here or in the area. They could be in the bedroom. I eased the door open and began to walk through.

Chapter 34: Rick

I heard Jordan shut the door and start the car. "That was a bit of strange luck."

"Whatever," I tried to focus on the impound. I thought about help not coming and somehow Jordan making it to African. Mrs. Simmons, Adrian, and myself–would accompany that psychopath. Why do good things sometimes happen to bad people? *Balance,* I thought. You wouldn't understand that in my position. The devil was sitting in the front seat.

I felt the car vibrate, and I heard motorcycles. I opened my eyes and counted six big guys on choppers. White Shield stitched on the back of their jackets. The bikes stopped at the bar, and the guys went inside. Jordan pulled into the lot and parked next to the Cadillac. Adrian was the first to get out, followed by Mrs. Simmons, then Jordan. I looked at the choppers from the backseat. *White Shield,* I thought. The name looked familiar. I'd seen the name before but couldn't put my finger on it.

"Get out," I heard Jordan on the outside of my window.

I looked at his face through the glass. He was seconds away from murdering a police officer, but his expression didn't show it. It's like he had an on and off switch he could use whenever he wanted. Nothing mattered to him. It's not easy to become an FBI agent. I wonder if Jordan had any regrets after switching sides? I got out of the car and looked Jordan in the eyes. I wanted to spit in his face for what he put me through ever since the warehouse. He smirked at me as I continued past him. I heard the car lock as I met Adrian and Mrs. Simmons at the front door.

"Hungry," It was something about the way Adrian asked that didn't sit right.

"Sure," I said sarcastically. I looked at Mrs. Simmons. Even though she decided to work with Jordan, I remained a gentleman. "After you," I said to her and slightly bowed. Adrian stepped inside next and then Jordan.

Jordan stopped next to me. He didn't look at my face when he said. "I'm watching you." Half a smile formed on the side of his face, and he continued past me.

The bartender was a woman. Her hair was silver and styled in a mohawk with the sides cut short—a spritz of red dye colored the tips front to back. She wore a sleeveless shirt, and I could see tattoos covering both arms. I scanned around the bar paranoid, looking for any signs of trouble. I sat down across from Jordan, next to Mrs. Simmons. Adrian sat beside him. The bikers like the attention they were getting, or they just enjoyed being wild and loud. There were a few other people in the bar, none more interesting than the bikers.

A woman with a bald head covered in tattoos, light blue lipstick, dark eyeliner, tennis skirt, and long black leather heels asked for our order. She looked around thirty, the same I thought about the bartender. She looked at the bikers and snarled at them in a distasteful manner.

I picked up the menu that was sitting on the table. I hadn't eaten since this morning, and my stomach was growling. "I'll take a-"

"He'll have a cheeseburger and a water," Jordan interrupted. "and the same for me. The woman across from me will have your best salad. And the asshole next to me is paying for everyone."

"Do you want fries with that," the waitress asked Jordan. "and a water for her?"

"Of course," Jordan said sarcastically.

A cheeseburger meal works for me. I knew what Jordan was trying to do. He wanted to limit conversation. I'd got a feeling that he wasn't happy about being here. Mrs. Simmons smiled, satisfied with her order. Adrian stared at Jordan. His face had no signs of being upset, and there was a cunning look in his eyes.

"Cheeseburger, fries," Adrian said and revealed my wallet. He handed my credit card to the waitress. "and the house beer."

"Beer for me," I said. Jordan had a pissed look on his face. "What, I'm paying for it."

"I'll have a one as well," Mrs. Simmons spoke up. "I take it you don't have wine."

The waitress looked at each of us and repeated the order. Jordan upgraded to the house beer like everyone else, and she left.

"You gonna keep that?" I said, looking at Adrian. He picked the wallet up and tossed it to me. "Do I need to check it?" I held it up for him to see. "Just fucking with you." I put the wallet away.

"Funny," Jordan said with a sarcastic look on his face. "Rick's the funniest guy I know." He slapped his knee.

"How sweet," Mrs. Simmons said, looking at Jordan.

Jordan matched her stare. The two of them had been going at each other's neck since the driving incident. I felt some tension between them. I could use it to my advantage. Jordan should have taken what I said about them coming up with a plan to betray him more seriously. They could murder him if it got that far. Something I shouldn't worry about, I wouldn't mind him dead.

"You forgot to mention this is a biker's bar," Jordan said, looking at Adrian.

"There were only a few people the last time I ate here," Adrian shot back.

"You should know better than that," Jordan said. "A place like this, and you didn't see any signs? Just look at the people working here." He put his elbows on the table and looked around the bar.

"Does it matter who eats here?" Mrs. Simmons said.

"Yes," Jordan held up his hand. "and I think we're the wrong color."

"C'mon," I said. "you're gonna play the race card?"

"That's easy for you to say," Jordan answered. "I busted a few members of White Shield back in the day. They don't take kindly to colored folks if you know what I mean."

"No," Adrian said. "I don't know what you mean. Would you like to explain?"

"Stop being a dick," Jordan sucked his teeth. "Where's my beer?"

"A minute ago, you wanted water," Adrian leaned back and crossed his leg over the other. "Now, you're crying about a beer."

The waitress came back to the table. She walked around and set our drinks in front of us. She told us our food would be ready soon.

"Right on time," I said, grabbing my beer and taking a sip. I needed it bad. I was in a bar with six racist bikers who are criminals, according to Jordan. I wasn't raised that way. I was taught the respect you give is the respect you get. Mrs. Simmons, Jordan, and Adrian were black. I stuck out like a sore thumb, not because I'm a white guy because I look like a cop.

I kept my eyes on the bikers while we waited for our food. The bikers had their eyes on us. They stopped being loud, which was strange for a few drunk men. I knew they were plotting a move. One of them could have recognized Jordan.

The food arrived, and we began to eat. Everyone except Jordan thanked the waitress. The burger was not bad, and the fries were salty but eatable. Jordan didn't look at us or the bikers while he ate. Mrs. Simmons was in her own world, paying attention to no one while eating her salad. Adrian kept his guard up. His eyes didn't show where he was looking, but I knew he had everyone in the bar under surveillance. I noticed he was using a knife and fork to eat his food. He cut into the burger and picked it up with his fork. I thought about the knife being secured in his hand while he ate was a safety precaution? That was something an assassin would do, keep a weapon on hand. I was watching Adrian when I heard a harsh voice over our table.

"Niggers not welcome," I looked up and saw one of the bikers. "especially, cops."

Chapter 35: Kane

We crept through the door cautiously, trying not to alert anybody on the other side. Smoke was right behind me. The room was dark, and I really couldn't see anything but what was in front of us. The inside was a nice size. You could tell the room cost a grip.

Smoke shut the door without making a sound. *So far, so good,* I thought. I aimed the gun in the direction I was moving. The main area came into full view. Nobody was in sight. It was quiet enough to hear Smoke breathing behind me. I stopped by a closet door. "Open it?"

Smoke held up three fingers and counted down, silently. He swiftly opened the door without making any noise.

I pressed the gun. "Good." I turned around and pointed at the couch. He nodded back, and I signed to the other side of the sofa. I watched him slowly move around to the location. I crept to the opposite end and signaled to act simultaneously. It was clear. I moved to the curtains and slid them open, no one there. "Do you think this the right room?" I began to think the cleaning ladies led us to a dead end. Maybe she was no longer staying in the room?

"We're about to find out," Smoke was looking at the bedroom door. "They gotta be making love for it to be this quiet."

"Right," I muttered and hurried to the side of the door and leaned against the surface. "Open it, and I'll go in first."

Smoke got in position and put his hand on the doorknob. He turned the knob until it made a faint clicking noise. "Fuck," He muttered.

I put my finger to my mouth. "Sh…" I listened for any sounds coming from inside the room. It was dead. I shrugged at Smoke. I guessed we were good because I didn't hear anybody. "Slowly," I whispered. Smoke began opening the door. I couldn't believe what I saw after looking inside. The scene was shocking, and I almost fired a shot. I blinked several times to make sure my eyes weren't deceiving me. I was looking at Samatha tied down on the bed with a gag in her mouth.

"What the fuck is going on?" Smoke aimed his weapon at Samatha. "She was just downstairs."

"Rick was right," I said to Smoke and walked around the bed. I removed the gag from Samatha's mouth. "The guy with the funny hair did this to you?" I looked into her eyes. She looked like she was about to fall asleep. I undid the bind on her left arm. "Get the other one," I told Smoke. She was free. I shook her shoulders, trying to keep her eyes open. "Are you ok?"

When she didn't respond, Smoke said. "It's obvious this bitch is on drugs."

"Or somebody drugged her," I suggested. My instincts kicked in, and I felt that something was wrong. "check the bathroom and guard the front door."

Smoke searched the rest of the area inside the bathroom. It was clear, and he walked out of the bedroom door.

I sighed, thinking about the situation with Samatha. The only person who could have done this is the guy she was standing with in the dining area. Someone sent him after her. I looked down at her and thought about what to do. Calling the cops wouldn't be ideal. What would they think? That I did this to her? I shifted her head in my arms and called her name. She tried to answer but couldn't get the words out, and I called her name again, only to get the same result. I propped her up against the bed to free my arms. I pulled out my phone.

"Kane," Kim answered. "is everything ok?"

She sounded worried, and I knew she would be considering what we were doing. "We're good," I said. I told her everything that was going on with Samatha. Kim gave me the answer I was looking for. "Thank you," and ended the line. "Ok," I muttered and put the phone back in my pocket. I picked Samatha up from the bed. She settled in my arms like a baby. I carried her gracefully to the bathroom and stopped at the door. It was enough space to put my foot inside and pull it open. I spent inside with Samatha maneuvering with the door.

191

The lights were on inside the bathroom. It was bigger than I thought. There was a marble tub in the center. Large, colorful candles aligned around it. I walked past the tub, heading towards the standup shower. The floor on the inside was marble, and the trim of the shower was gold plated. There was a small TV on the wall next to it. I noticed it was on the news. I opened the shower door and gently sat Samatha down. I left all of her clothes on when I turned on the water. She started to move her head around. Kim said a cold shower would help, and it seemed to be working. Samatha was regaining consciousness. It was like magic when she opened her eyes. The water slapped against her face, and she held her arms up, blocking it.

Samatha's teeth began to chatter. She gripped her shoulders, shivering, and closed her eyes. She put her head down, and her hair dropped below her face, covering it.

"Samatha," I said. She was in trouble, and I wanted to know why. Rick knew this would happen to her. Lucky for her, we got here in time. I listened to the sound of water slap against her dress. I turned off the shower so I could hear if she spoke. She didn't respond because she was cold. I looked around the bathroom and found the closet. I hurried over and grabbed a towel. Drying her off helped warm her body. I began with her shoulders and then blotted her face, hands, and hair until she was dry enough to speak. "What happened?"

She had an innocent look in her eyes. "Who are you?"

"A friend of Rick," I told her.

Her eyes searched for an answer. "Rick, the policeman?"

"Yes," I said while helping her from the shower. "he sent me." I handed her another towel to dry herself. I got the impression she believed me.

"Rick is the reason this happened to me," she asked.

"I'm not sure," I said. "That's what I'm here to find out." I guided her into the bedroom so we could talk. "Rick called me and said you would be in danger. I don't know how he knew you would be, but I think there's a connection with my father."

"I don't know who your father is," she said. "I've slept with a lot of guys who didn't use their real names. It wouldn't surprise me if your father were protecting his identity from public embarrassment. That's how must senators and other congressmen handle our arrangements."

Did my father cheat on my mother with Samantha, I thought. He would never do anything to hurt his family. Samantha had to be involved with him in another way. "I don't believe you slept with my father. Rick wasn't clear about why you were in danger. The guy you were with earlier."

She interrupted. "He did this to me," she looked down at her feet. "I met him in the lobby. I thought he was a nice guy. He paid upfront for my services. Everything was fine until..." she began to sob.

The man was the danger Rick spoke of on the phone. At least for now, she was safe. I approached, interrogating her from another angle. "How are you and Rick connected?"

"Rick," Samantha's voice was at a whisper. "he's the nicest man in the world and a client of mine. We were together last night. He left this morning while I was asleep."

"Did he mention anything to you about his ex-partner?" I asked.

"The black guy he's obsessed with," she stopped crying. "Jordan, the one who betrayed him?"

"Yes," I said. "you know him?"

"Never met him," she said. "Rick talked about him a lot after what happened."

"At the warehouse," I asked.

"Yes," she answered. "that's all he ever talks about these days. It's kind of sad, but that's what comes with my job. Listening to the problems people have as if I don't have any of my own."

"Has he ever mentioned anything about a gun smuggler?" I asked evenly, trying to hide what my father was. I wanted to keep that bit of information safe. It wasn't public, so she didn't need to know.

"No," she sat on the edge of the bed. "I don't know anything about guns or anyone smuggling them. Is that why the guy came after me?"

"No," I replied.

"Then why asked?" she said incredulously.

"Trying to find an answer," I said. There was something I missed. I couldn't find a connection between Samantha and my father. It had to be something else. "How long have you and Rick known each other?"

"Five years," she looked down at her hands. "he wants me to stop. He told me a time or two that this line of work isn't safe. Pretty girls like me marry rich men and start a family. I should've listened to him."

Five years, I thought. I took into consideration that it was more than enough time for Jordan to find out about Samantha. He could be using her to threaten Rick. It was clear to me from what Samantha said that Rick cares for her. If I could figure it out, so could Jordan. Right then, I realized that I hit another dead end. Samantha couldn't do anything for me. Although, we did make good on saving her for Rick's sake.

"What was that?" Samantha had a worried looked on her face. She stood up from the bed terrified and backed up against the wall. "It's him."

"There's nothing to worry about," I assured her. "I'm not alone. My friend is out there." I walked to the door. Samantha didn't move from the wall as I opened it and called his name. "Smoke, you good?" I got no response. "Smoke," I called again. No answer. I turned to Samantha and signaled for her to hide somewhere. I pulled out my gun and peeped into the living area of the room. I didn't hear or see Smoke anywhere. "Fuck," I muttered. I got distracted and left Smoke alone for too long. If the guy got to Smoke, that meant he was still hiding in the room after we entered. The question was, how did we miss him? I crept around the room, searching every angle. The lights were still off, and I thought about turning them on. I checked behind the small bar. "Smoke," he was out cold. His gun was on the ground next to him. I bent down and propped him up against the bar cabinets. As I got Smoke situated, I felt the barrel of a gun pressed against the back of my head. I knew I was dead after hearing gunfire.

Chapter 36: Abel

After my conversation with Snake and Bam, Gina and Britt came downstairs. There was enough tension in the room between Britt and Gina that the house could have gone up in flames. That's how intense it was sitting there in silence. Gina sat on my lap, and I knew it was to piss off Britt. I refused to make Gina get up even though her weight caused pain to my ribs. That would have only gotten her angry, and who knows what she would do next. My goal was to keep her in a happy place until we made it to Africa, where I would get rid of Silva and Britt.

"Why are you looking at her like you want to kill her?" Bam asked Gina. He was still watching the news on the TV.

"Because I do," Gina smiled at him.

Britt didn't say anything in response to Gina. She knew what Gina would do to her if she did.

Snake shook his head. "Why don't you leave her be?"

"Wait," Gina stood from my lap. "you both are defending her. I get it. The both of you want to fuck her. Of course, a typical guy crush with his dick," she looked at Britt. "You better watch out."

I took the opportunity to stand. "I need to get some fresh air," I said before walking out to the balcony. I was in the same spot as before, looking over at Silva's place. The patio light was off, meaning the plan was not yet ready. *How much longer do I have to wait,* I thought. Silva should have gotten it fueled by now. Did he not care for Britt and took the chance to escape?

"Why are you acting so kind to her?" It was Gina. I heard her approach from behind. "Is she that special?"

I turned around and met her stare. "No," I answered. "the only special person I know is you, my love." She fell into my arms, and I got tense from the pain.

"I'm sorry," Gina said. "I forgot," she released her hold around my neck after kissing me on the lips.

"It's ok," I said. "you don't have to worry about Britt after we get to Africa. We won't need them after we touchdown. I went over what I need from Snake and Bam. They're aware of what has to be done."

Gina smiled at me, and it didn't seem fake. There are times when I had to ask myself if I could trust her. And every time, she had come through for me. She stood beside me with her arms on the ledge of the balcony, watching the night sky over the ocean. It was beautiful. The type of view people thought of as romantic. A sight you share with the person you love. To me, it was the last thing you want to see before you die—something beyond your reach that could bring light to any person with a

198

dark heart. Gina was the brightest star in the sky, and I was the ocean. Nothing could come between us, only space.

"It's magnificent," she looked memorized by the endless view of the ocean, steaming along the water as they met far off in the distance.

"That it is," I said. "you see where the ocean and the sky meet?"

"I do," Gina's voice was pleasant, and she leaned her head against my shoulder.

"That's how you get to heaven," I said. That was the only thing that ever interested me Jar had said when I was just a boy. I was intrigued by what he meant by it. Now that I'm older, I know.

"Then no would ever make it there alive," she said.

I smiled, "That's the point. Only when you pass away that you're allowed to walk to the ends of the earth. People like me don't make it. We're imprisoned on this planet, walking the same path for eternity without anybody to love."

"I don't mind walking with you," she said. "even if we're lost for eternity. We'll still be together."

I looked down and kissed the top of her forehead. "That would be nice," I said as the light on Silva's patio turned on.

Chapter 37: Jordan

"Niggers not welcome," I heard a voice call me out of my name from behind. "especially, cops." It was one of the bikers standing over me.

I turned back around and looked at Adrian. Things were about to get dirty. I felt it when we walked in. White Shield is the successor to the infamous biker gang, Hell's Angels. They were equally if not more dangerous. In my time dealing with the club, there were hundreds of members spread across the map. Their numbers have indeed grown to the thousands since then. We were lucky to only run into a few members of their organization.

The bikers formed a circle around our table. The gang leader who spoke now stood over Noti, or whatever the hell name she wants me to call her. He bent low and got close to her ear. His long beard brushed against the side of her neck and shoulder. "I've never been with a nigger before. This one is actually purdy."

Noti didn't move. The look on her face didn't express any signs of fear. "I would advise you to remove yourself clear of my space," she said in a calm and controlled manner.

Rick spoke up. "Why don't you guys leave." He opened his wallet and set it in the center of the table.

"FBI," the leader laughed, and the other members joined in on the fun. "Look where ya at? A badge means nothing in these parts."

What the fuck are you doing, Rick? Threatening a member of White Shield with a badge will only get you killed.

I didn't teach him enough when we were together. It was another rookie mistake on his end. Adrian gave me a look that said he was ready for action. Just thinking about his skills, he could take them out alone. But where would the excitement be in that?

Rick leaned back in his chair. "This is your last warning."

"Whadda ya gonna do," the leader snarled. "take us to jail?" The bikers all laughed at Rick.

Before I could react, Notie grabbed a fork and stuck it in the leader's eye.

"Ah," the biker roared and stumbled back off balance while trying to pull out the fork. "ya black bitch!"

It was time to have some fun. I could use a warmup before the impound. The bikers attacked us all at once. One grabbed my shoulder, and before he knew it, a beer bottle shattered over his skull. He held his head and bent over, yelling at the floor in pain. I picked up the chair I was sitting in and crushed it over the biker's back, causing him to fall on his stomach. My shoe came down on the back of his head. I wanted to see if I could smash his brains into the floor. "That's for interrupting my meal," I said before something heavy struck across my spine. "Ah," I fell to the ground and turned on my backside to defend off the attacker.

"Ya gonna die, nigger," another biker held a gun in my face.

I reacted by kicking the weapon out of his hand. I watched his eyes trail off behind the gun. He had a look of disbelief on his face after having the advantage. I reached for my weapon and waited for the biker's attention. His eyes grew two sizes bigger when he noticed the gun. He didn't have a chance.

Boom!

That was the end of him. There was nothing attached to his shoulders as I watched his lifeless body fall over. I got up and couldn't believe what I saw. Adrian was sitting down at the table, eating like nothing ever happened.

"You're rusty," he said and bit his burger.

Chapter 38: Rick

"Whadda ya gonna do," the biker looked at me from over the shoulder of Mrs. Simmons. "take us to jail?" The bikers began to laugh, and before anyone could react. Mrs. Simmons poked him in the eye with a fork.

"Ah," the biker roared and backed off Mrs. Simmons.

I had to react to what happened quickly. The biker began crying out in pain, trying to remove the fork from the socket of his eye. He was successful, and I watched him throw the silverware on the floor. We were face to face in a staredown. He was panting hard, and I could see his massive chest heave in breaths of air. It was on. The biker charged at me with a ferocious glare in his eyes. Adrian took me by surprise. He swiftly maneuvered in front of me, blocking the biker from my view. It appeared to me they were locked in a bearhug. The biker's head rested on Adrian's left shoulder. His good eye began to fade, and blood leaked out of the socket from his other eye. He released his hold around Adrian. His body suddenly dropped to the ground like a bag of photos. I heard his head thump on the floor.

My attention was back on Adrian, and he turned around to face me. My mind couldn't register how fast he'd moved on the biker. *What could I do with a guy like him,* I thought. Suddenly, he reached for something on his side and threw it in my direction. I got scared, thinking he was about to take me out with the rest of them.

"Ah," I heard a cry of agony from behind.

It was another biker. The object Adrian had thrown was the same dagger he'd drew on me in the woods. The biker held his neck, looking up at the ceiling, and stumbled around with weak legs. Adrian rushed over and removed his blade. Blood gushed between the biker's hands, and he fell dead on the floor. The dragger flew past my head again. I began to think Adrian like terrify me by putting me in the crossfire. I tried to follow the dagger through the air with my eyes.

The blade entered the chest of another biker, right over his heart. "Fucking…nigg-"

Adrian was on the biker before he could get the word out. He thrust the blade deeper inside the biker's heart. He stood there stunned, keeping eye contact with Adrian as he passed. Adrian sat the biker in a nearby chair and backed away.

Boom!

I ducked for cover, reacting to gunfire. I looked around and saw Jordan on the floor with a gun. One of the bikers stood over him with an enormous chunk of meat missing from his head. The inside of the biker's skull looked gruesome. I'd never in my life seen an actual brain until today. It was something I would always remember. I crawled under the table to protect myself in need of a weapon. I heard a yelp but couldn't identify where it came from with all the noise in my ear. Someone sat at the table, and it caused me to move from cover.

"You're rusty," I heard Adrian's voice as I stood up. Surprisingly, he was sitting at the table eating his burger.

"Where is she?" Jordan growled.

I looked at Adrain, and he held up three fingers at Jordan.

"Fuck," Jordan obviously knew what that meant.

Mrs. Simmons was missing along with the last biker. It was a terrible situation. I searched around the bar, looking for her, and so did Jordan. Adrian continued to enjoy his food.

"Help," I heard Mrs. Simmons cry out.

I looked at the entrance and spotted the biker holding Mrs. Simmons captive. He grabbed her by the waist hostage, leaving the bar. Jordan and I rushed over. I stepped out of the building into the parking lot. The biker was moving towards the motorcycles. Mrs. Simmons struggled the entire time, trying to free herself.

"Ya come any closer," the biker got in position by an all-chrome chopper with ghost flames on the tank. "I'll kill this filth."

Jordan held his gun up to the biker. "That wouldn't be a wise decision." He slowly closed in on the target.

I didn't have a weapon. Jordan and Adrian deprived me of that. Even so, I closed in with Jordan.

"Ya stay right there, nigger," the biker got his motorcycle started, and the engine roared to life. He reached in the saddle while keeping his eyes on us. It was a long barrel .357 magnum.

Not good, I thought. Mrs. Simmons elbowed the biker in his gut, and he released her. The biker kept the gun aimed at us after letting Mrs. Simmons escape. He got on his chopper and kicked the stand. Mrs. Simmons had reached us by then and hid behind me. Jordan focused on the biker, and so did I. The chopper began to pull off when it suddenly exploded. A cloud of black smoke filled the air like a nuclear aftereffect. I covered my mouth to keep smoke from entering my lungs.

What happened? That was the only thing that came to mind.

Jordan didn't pull the trigger. I would have known because I was beside him. I turned around and spotted the bartender with the red tip mohawk. She had a rifle in her hands.

She looked at us and smiled. "They were rude to my girlfriend."

Chapter 39: Kane

I felt a gun pressed to the back of my head. I heard gunfire, and my reaction was too slow. I was a dead man. A loud thump hit the floor, and I turned around and saw a body. It was the man with the funny hair. Thankfully, I was still alive. He was rolling around on the floor, holding his hand.

"My hand," the gunman cried out in pain.

I got up and looked at the bedroom door, thinking Samantha had saved my life.

"You good," I heard Bear to my left.

I saw Bear and Big Bruce standing by the entrance. They hurried over to me. "Yeah."

"What's up with him?" Big Bruce asked.

"Don't know," I picked up a Sig P365, a small-caliber pistol. It belonged to the gunman.

"My hand," the gunman continued to throw a fit while he held his hand.

"What happened to Smoke," Bear asked.

"This guy," I kicked him on the side of his chest out of frustration. He got me pissed at what he did to Smoke.

"Lemme get some," Bear kicked the guy hard enough to flip him over.

"Might as well," Big Bruce joined in and booted the guy across the room. If it weren't for the couch blocking the way, the gunman would've kept sliding across the floor.

"Good foot," I said, amazed by how far Bruce kicked the gunman.

"I'll grab Smoke," Bear offered. "you two can deal with him." he concealed his gun and hoisted Smoke from the floor.

I walked over to funny hair, and Bruce followed me. The gunman acted like he was about to die. A gunshot wound to the hand and three kicks to the chest wouldn't kill anybody of age. Unless they went into shock or something, but that wasn't the case with the gunman. "Yo," I called to him. "you're cryin' like a fuckin' baby. It's not that serious."

"This is the worst pain I've ever felt," funny hair looked mentally destroyed. Snot ran down his nose; sweat covered his funny-looking hair and forehead. His sharp suit was now a wrinkled mess. His eyes had the look of defeat in them.

"Whatever," I said incredulously.

The gunman held up his hand, and half of his fingers were gone.

"Damn..." Bruce and I said simultaneously.

Bruce spoke up. "Put that thing away." He covered his mouth and showed signs of wanting to vomit. "Dat shit nasty."

"You did this to me," the gunman said hysterically.

"Can you find something to wrap his hand in?" I asked Bruce.

"No problem," Bruce went off.

"Three things," I told the gunman. "One, you're not gonna die. Two, who sent you? Three, why?"

The gunman looked into my eyes and began to laugh through his cries. "You won't get a thing out of me. I've killed more people than you know."

I'd figured this guy was a maniac when he began to sob earlier. Something had to be wrong with this guy if Jordan did send him. *Birds of a feather flock together,* I thought.

Bruce came back with a rag. "He can wrap this around it for now," he held it out.

"Nah," I said with sarcasm. "he won't need that where he's going. I thought about it and decided he's useless. We should toss him over the balcony. Whadda think?"

"Whatever," Bruce shrugged.

"You're not a killer," funny hair said. "I can tell by the look in your eyes."

"That's the thing you don't get," I said with a sinister smile. "it's called consistently. Who do you think killed Ke'Mo Cutt?"

The gunman's eyes grew wide. "Ke'Mo was a trained killer like myself," He started laughing louder. "lies...all lies. He shot himself in the head. Everybody knows that."

This guy reminded me of the Joker with his funny hair and the way he laughs. I knew what I had to do with him. I had all the information that I needed from him. If I left him alive, someone else would die. He wouldn't stop. Jordan only rolls with killers, and that's what I had to become to survive. It was the same feeling I got before the bank job. Something deep down inside of my mind told me to change and become that dread-headed monster. That guy who didn't give a fuck and would do anything for his family. This lunatic, laughing like a madman in my face…had to be eliminated.

I grabbed a handful of the gunman's shirt over his chest. I began to drag him across the floor. "Bruce, get the balcony door."

Bruce hurried over and to open it.

"Wha…what are you doing?" the gunman cried. "you think I'm afraid to die?" He laughed. "you still don't know who sent me."

"The Planner," I said down at him.

"But why is what you need to know," he said and continued laughing. "and you'll never know the answer."

I got him out of the room and onto the balcony. I picked him up like a puppy and held him against the ledge. "Samatha, the girl he sent you to watch. I know this because she would've been dead when I found her. Therefore, that gave you a reason to wait. She's connected with the detective. Jordan needs something and used her to threaten him. That part was easy to figure out after speaking to her. When I said you were useless, I meant it."

"Well done," the gunman said. "I'm useless. Go ahead and toss me over," he laughed. "I'm ready to die."

"You were crying about your hand five seconds ago," Bruce said. "and now you're ready to die?"

The gunman looked at Bruce and smiled. He nodded his head as if he lost his mind and raised his damaged hand. "The pain is gone."

"He's a psychopath," I told Bruce. I looked at the gunman. "He's a murderer—a serial killer who enjoys taking the lives of others. Look at him. He's sick, and there is nothing that would make him better. Myself, Samantha, and Smoke would all be dead if you didn't intervene. He wouldn't have stopped there. More innocent people would've died by his hands. That's the way of life. Good guys and bad guys."

"Which are you?" funny hair asked with a grin.

I looked deep into his eyes and didn't see a grin or even a snicker. A more serious look took over his face. He was terrified, and that was how I wanted him to feel. "A monster," I answered and pushed him over the ledge.

Chapter 40: Jordan

Noti elbowed the biker and scampered off behind Rick. I kept the gun on the biker as he got on his chopper and began to pull off. I had a decision to make. I could hold my position or shoot to kill. If the biker got off a good shot and killed Notie or Rick, my plan would go to shit. I couldn't risk the fool killing one of them. In the next instant, the motorcycle erupted in flames behind a loud explosion. I was confused, thinking Adrian had rigged the bikes before we walked in. But that would be putting thoughts in my head that wasn't true. We had all walked in together. I looked at Rick, thinking he'd done this, and he appeared focused on something else.

I heard a woman's voice. "They were rude to my girlfriend."

It was the bartender with the arm tatts and silver mohawk. She held an M13 assault rifle with a scope in her hands. I put my gun away and approached her. "It's a shame you're gay," I said, looking in her eyes and moving down to her chest. She wore a sleeveless shirt styled with an open-cut middle, showing off her perky breasts.

"Lesbian," she corrected seductively and used her free hand to trace her finger around the lining of her boobs.

"Nice butterfly tatt," I said, moving in closer to her. The tattoo covered her breasts. The body of the insect was in the center, and the wings filled the sides.

She pulled open her shirt a little to show more of her right tit. "Do you wanna see the rest of it?" She moved in and gently kissed the side of my neck.

"Bring the gun," I said.

In the next thirty seconds, we made our way into the women's restroom. We were going at each other like lovers for the first time. I didn't care what idiot Rick, nagging Noti, or my dickhead brother was doing. I had to have this woman right here and now. It'd been too long since I last held a woman in my arms. She felt like a drug. I kicked through the stall at the end. We entered, and she shut the door.

She pulled her shirt over her head. "I hope it's like they say it is," she pulled her tiny skirt up and lifted her leg, exposing her private area.

"Oh, it is," I said, getting my pants down and exposing myself. I took it as she'd never been with a black guy. Well, she was about to get a full load. I inserted myself and grabbed a hand full of her left breast.

"Oh," she moaned after a deep thrust hit her pelvis. "It's so big." She squeezed both of my shoulders.

I tried to kill her with each thrust. She didn't weigh much, and every pump lifted her body. We were in a rhyme, thrust, lift, moan, descend. The Planner was giving it to this bitch, and I felt like a man again. It's insane what pussy could do to a man.

"Give me that fuckin' dick harder," she said and let out a loud moan. Her tongue was incredibly long, and she licked her right breast. "choke me."

She grabbed my hand and put it around her neck. I squeezed, and I felt in control as I began to sweat. I watched her tits bounce in my face. Her pink nipples were hard, and it turned me on. I had one hand on her neck and the other on her leg to keep a sturdy position. I lowered my head and took a mouth full of breasts, kissing all around them.

She had an unhappy look on her face when I pulled out. "No," she cried.

"Shut up, bitch," I turned her around and flipped up her skirt. I pounded her hardcore doggy style. Both of her hands were on the stall door for support. I grabbed the back of her neck and waist. She moaned every time my pelvis slapped against her ass. She looked back at me, and the expression on her face said I was the king. I noticed dragon tattoos covering her back, along with a bunch of Chinese symbols and writing. The only thing I understood was the text on her left ass cheek that read, *slap here.* I did several times. I was actually enjoying myself. I haven't had this much fun since the warehouse shootout with the fucking Africans. I got infuriated thinking about it and spaced out. I used more force each time I slapped her ass. The grip I had around her neck tightened. *Fucking Africans,* I thought.

Fucking Rick...fucking Kane. I didn't know what I was doing anymore. She ceased all movement and collapsed on the bathroom floor. I looked down at her and saw that she was dead.

I killed her...

"I'm cumming!"

I heard a voice and snapped back to reality. I was still fucking the woman with the silver mohawk. I didn't kill her, and that surprised me because it felt like I had.

"Shit, shit, shit.." she repeated as her body began to shake.

I felt the same sensation, and my legs got weaker. It was time to end the session, and I erupted inside of her. "Ah," I moaned, and my legs stiffened until it was all out. I sighed, relaxing my body and moving back.

"That was amazing," she said, fixing herself. "Don't worry. I can't get pregnant."

Chapter 41: Kane

I heard the gunman scream the entire way down until he collided with the pavement. I looked over the balcony. "Wha the?" I had to question myself. I also blinked a couple of times to make sure my eyes weren't playing tricks on me. I'd thought I saw the gunman move his arm, but it could have been his brain causing the nerves to twitch. I heard about people who had died and still had enough brain activity to move at the funeral while in their casket. That would be some scary shit to witness.

I shrugged it off and didn't think twice about pushing him over. The gunman would have never stopped coming for me. Jordan would have made sure of it. What I have to do is terminate anybody affiliated with Jordan. That's the only way to end his madness. Ke'Mo Cutt, and now this guy. I could only imagine what other lunatics were working with Jordan.

"Damn," Bruce said. "I didn't think you had it in you."

I looked at Bruce and stepped back inside. Bruce was now a part of this after witnessing what I'd done. He needed to know how far I would go if someone forced my hand. In his mind, I'm a murderer. That was his first time seeing anything like that. When he covered his mouth after seeing the blood on the gunman's hand, I knew he was fresh. I took care of business and planted a seed in Bruce's head that said, don't cross Kane.

To be apart of this crew, that's how you have to get down. I'd already lost Redd, one of my best friends. And I'll be damned if I lose someone else I care about.

Bear and Smoke were sitting on the couch. Smoke had a bag of ice on his head. I walked over to him. "What happened?"

He looked up at me and sighed. "I came out of the room and walked to the front door. When I got by the bar, I was struck in the back of my head. He had to be in the room already. Mufucka was probably using the bar for cover. The only place we didn't check." Smoke stood up. "Man, you shoulda let me toss his punk ass over," he said, frustrated at himself.

The bedroom door opened, and Samantha walked out. She looked terrified.

"It's ok," I held up my hand to her. "They're with me."

She looked relieved that they weren't a threat. "Did you get him?"

I signed at her that I took care of it without telling her the specifics. "You have to leave this hotel immediately. The police will be swarming around her soon, asking questions. Find a friend, family member, or somebody you trust to stay with for a while. I don't know if Jordan will send someone else after you."

"Wait," she said. "who are you?"

217

It didn't take long for me to give her an answer. "I told you, a friend of Rick." I rounded up the boys. It was time for us to blow this joint. We got to the door, and I was the last to leave.

"Thank you," Samantha smiled at me.

I nodded and smiled back, and then she closed the door. I was glad for that to be over and done. Danger was still ahead, and that was only a slice of it. My life was at stake at every turn of the page. I was living the life of an action hero in a graphic novel. But in this story, I'm the author.

I stepped into the hall with my crew. "Let's try not to set off any alarms while getting out of here. You two leave back out together. Smoke, and I will take the stairs. Pick us up at the corner on the main street. We dapped each other and bounced.

Bear pushed the button for the elevator, and they got on. Smoke and I headed for the stairs. We got back to the main lobby of the hotel. There were all kinds of commotion going on around us. It wasn't pandemonium or anything close. The people around us were more interested in what was taking place outside. That's where most of the people inside of the lobby started to migrate. I knew what it was when I first saw how they were acting. They were reacting to the gunman. I imagined his body mangled and twisted in an unorthodox manner. It was a horrific way to die.

"C'mon," I led Smoke through the crowd of people. Nobody paid attention to us as we exited the hotel. I looked over to the group observing the gunman. They were aligned directly in our path to the corner. *Man,* I thought. *No sweat.* We walked up to the crowd. I didn't desire to not look because who wouldn't be nosey at this moment? We had to act like everyone else to get by without being suspect. I looked down at funny hair and was shocked at what I saw.

"You failed," the gunman said. He laughed and coughed out blood. "you failed to kill me!"

I looked at Smoke, and his expression was the same as mine. How could he be alive? The room was on the third floor. It didn't seem that far up after looking at it from this vantage point. I guessed you could survive a fall like that if you didn't land head first. He must have broken his legs from the fall, at least. It would keep him out of commission for a while.

Suddenly, the gunman spotted me through the crowd. "You failed," he laughed. "you failed to take my life!"

I'd glance around and saw a few eyes on me. No one had figured out funny hair was speaking about me.

"Let's move," Smoke said. "Before the police get here."

"Right," I said in a low tone, still in shock that the gunman was able to survive. We left the scene before someone decided to play detective and point me out of the group. We made it to the corner. Bear pulled the Humvee around in the nick of time. Police vehicles began to flood the area as we got inside the truck.

"You guys won't believe this," Bear said after we shut both doors. "dude survived."

"Yeah," I said from the backseat. "he was talking shit when we walked past."

"Same with us," Bruce commented.

"Maybe he'll turn into a fuckin' zombie," Smoke said. "so I can kill his ass a few more times."

Smoke had to be pissed off to say something like that. I didn't blame him. The gunman managed to get the drop on him. Guys don't like to lose at anything and then get it thrown in your face with shit talk is below ground level. The gunman kind of got me pissed as well. I began to think I couldn't kill these maniacs Jordan got working for him. I was a split second away from killing Ke'Mo, and he took his own life. Then, funny hair survived a fucking fall from three stories. *What next?* These guys were like supervillains.

"Where to," Bear asked and turned the block onto the next street.

I sighed and leaned my head back on the headrest. A ton of shit was on my mind. I had to sort through the mess and focus on the main objective. Rick mentioned the police impound.

Jordan was planning to steal a plane. *That's where I need to be,* I thought. "The police impound."

Chapter 42: Rick

Jordan and the mohawk lady got really close. I couldn't hear what they were talking about. Whatever was going on between them just went up a notch. I saw mohawk kiss Jordan on the neck, which I thought was strange and unexpected when it happened. The two didn't look like they belonged together. Now, I beg to differ. She came out of nowhere and blew a guy to kingdom come with an M13. She didn't match with Jordan, but The Planner was her guy. They fit perfectly together.

"What are they doing?" Mrs. Simmons said, watching Jordan and mohawk makeout.

"The question is," I said after the kissing pair entered the bar. "where are they heading to do what I think they're gonna do?" *Wait a minute,* I thought. Jordan and Adrian were inside the bar, leaving me the perfect opportunity to go for my phone. I hurried over to the car. I didn't have much time before Mrs. Simmons knew what I was up to. If I had the keys, I would've driven off and forced Mrs. Simmons to go with me. I got to the vehicle and punched the code in the number pad on the door. Mrs. Simmons was on my ass the moment she heard the door open.

"What are you doing?" She asked over my shoulder.

"Don't worry," I said. "I can't drive off without the key." I bent down to check under the driver seat where I lost the phone. I felt around on the floorboard. *Got it.* The phone was in my hand, and I didn't have a lie cooked up for Mrs. Simmons after learning she's with them. I retracted my arm and stood. A tiny amount of pain spread through my back. I couldn't help getting old, so I had to stretch.

"You are not leaving," Mrs. Simmons told me. "And you're not using that phone." She tried to reach for it.

I held the phone away and fought her off until she stopped trying to reach for it. "I'm not leaving, and you're not getting this phone."

"Fine," she backed off.

I spoke up quickly because I thought she was about to snitch. "I'm not calling the cops."

"Why did you get the phone if not?" She questioned.

"I want to make sure Samantha is safe," I partly told her the truth. I wanted to correct my mistake from earlier when I called her son by accident. And it didn't seem likely Mrs. Simmons was about to let me call the cops either. "The woman Jordan threatened to kill if I didn't cooperate. I promise, no funny stuff." I put on the most innocent facial expression I could manage. "Please, trust me. I just want to make sure she's safe."

Mrs. Simmons looked around and not in a worried kind of way but curious. "Ok, but hurry and I get the phone after. If they find it on you, you're dead."

"You got it," I found Cherry's name and pressed send.

"Rick," she answered, sounding troubled.

"It's me," I said. "Are you safe?"

"I am now," she assured me. "A black guy with dreadlocks saved me. He mentioned you two are friends."

"Kane," I muttered by mistake. I saw Mrs. Simmons do a full spin when I said her son's name. She put on a face that expressed she didn't want to inform Kane of her presence. That's the vibe I'd got from her. If Kane saved Cherry, that meant he doesn't want just to save his mother. He wants Jordan for himself. *Crazy fucking kid,* I thought. *Why didn't he listen?*

"What is going on Rick," Cherry cried. "why are people trying to kill me?"

"I'll explain later," I replied and turned my back to Mrs. Simmons. She kept distracting me by signing to end the call. "right now, I need you to go somewhere safe. I'll reach out to-" A powerful shot to my lower back interrupted me, and I dropped the phone. I reluctantly got spun around and faced Adrian. He didn't say a word and flashed a grin. His swift punch combos did all of the talking. The blows dealt enough damage to drop me. I ended up on the ground next to the phone. Dust and dirt covered my face and got inside my mouth. I heard Mrs. Simmons in the background cry out, that's enough. How thoughtful of her to be worried about me. Now that I think about

224

it. What she was trying to do was warn me of Adrian. I didn't listen, and that got my ass kicked. I heard Cherry call my name several times through the receiver. Adrian crushed the phone with one stomp. I laid on the ground, helpless, and my eyes closed, knowing I wouldn't get another chance. I could live with that now that I know Cherry was safe.

Chapter 43: Jordan

I pulled up my pants and walked out of the stall. I could have murdered Ms. Mohawk.

"See you around," she said as I got to the door.

I stopped and looked at her from the corner of my eyes. She was fixing herself in the mirror. "Sure you will." I pushed through the door. The first thing I noticed was Mohawk's girlfriend dragging a dead biker through the back door. I stopped to see what she was up to. I peeped outside and saw a pile of bodies. She began to pour gasoline over the pile, and then she tossed the container to the side. I raised my eyebrows, thinking both women were tough as nails. I watched the bikers go up in flames. I eased back into the bar. Adrian and the others were no longer at the table. His plate was empty. *Fuck,* I thought. *They left me. Sonofvabitch.* I powered walked to the front entrance. Adrian and Noti fucked me. I kicked through the front door out of frustration.

"That's enough," Noti grabbed Adrian's arm.

I sat there, confused at what was happening. Rick obviously took a beating, and Noti was trying to stop it. Suddenly, Adrian brought his leg up, ready to crush Rick's head. I rushed over and slid to a stop. I had my hands up, trying to bring things to a halt. It was too late. Adrian's boot came down but not on Rick. He stomped on a device next to Rick's head.

Adrian stared into my eyes. "Done having fun?"

I snarled at him. I couldn't be angry because I was thinking with my dick. I left Adrian alone to watch after Rick and Noti. It was after I saw the empty table that I'd realized my mistake. "When was the last time you had some fun?"

"Don't start, you two," Noti stepped between us.

I sighed and looked down at Rick. "What happened here?"

"He had a phone," Adrian said.

I bent down and retrieved what was left of the device. "I should have known." The screen got shattered, so there wasn't a way to find out who Rick contacted. I threw the phone across the street into the woods. "Did you find out who he was talking with?"

Adrian shook his head and looked at Noti. "She was out here when he made the call."

I looked at her. "You let him do it?"

"He didn't call the police," she said. "I tried to stop him."

"Who did he call?" I asked. "You have to know something?"

"He didn't get through," Noti kept a straight face. I couldn't tell if she was lying or not. "Your brother stopped him in time."

"Where did the phone come from?" Adrian asked Noti.

"He got it from the car after Jordan went back inside the bar." She replied. "If you wouldn't have been thinking about yourself. This wouldn't have happened." She looked away, turning her face to the side.

"You didn't check the car thoroughly," I told Adrian.

"And whose fault was that?" Adrian shot back. "You were in the vehicle with him. It would have helped if you kept an eye on him. Father taught you better than that. If you couldn't watch him, how are we going to survive in Africa?"

"You can twist it however you want," I said. "He wouldn't put his whore's life in danger by calling the cops. We have to get to the police impound. If he contacted the feds, they're gonna be all over the lot searching for us. In which case, we should be able to spot them if we move ahead of schedule."

Adrian helped Rick off the ground. "We'll take the police vehicle and leave the Cadillac. We don't have a use for it anymore."

I watched Adrian get Rick in the car. Noti had a worried look on her face. "You're lucky Adrian stopped him in time, or this thing we got going on would've been for nothing. Don't make a mistake like that if you wanna get through this alive." I left her there to think about what I said. I got in the car and sat in the driver's seat. Adrian got Rick inside and sat in the back with him. Notie was still standing on the outside, lost in thought. "C'mon," I blew the horn. He hurried around to the passenger side and got in. I started the engine and drove to the police impound.

Chapter 44: Kane

We drove away from the hotel. I had to get my mind ready for the unknown. Anything could happen at the police impound. It was the only option I had left. I could have called the FBI like Rick asked me to. They wouldn't have responded in time to save my mother. Jordan wasn't after the money I took from him. He was after a much larger payday, my father's safehouse. Using my mother was the only way to get it. One thing I had on my side was the police. We're driving to a government building, and if my knowledge serves me correct, there should be officers working on site. They should be more than enough help.

"I haven't been with you guys one day, and a guy got thrown from a third-floor balcony," Bruce said from the front seat. He looked back at me. "Is this how it is every day?"

I met Bruce's stare. What was I gonna say to him? He experienced what I'm cable of when I became a monster. It was a side of me I discovered at my lowest point. That was when I learned how to survive amongst creatures more inhuman than myself.

"If you can't handle the heat," Smoke spoke up. "Get your scary ass out of the kitchen."

Bruce adjusted in the seat to look at Smoke. "Nah, I like it." He turned around and left it at that.

Bear turned the corner and stopped at the next light. "What's the plan when we get there?"

I didn't have an answer off-top. It's been on my mind since I left the hotel. "I don't have a full-proof plan. Right now, I'm winging it. I figured we scope the place out and see if there's any suspicious activity. Jordan and Adrian are wanted criminals. He can't walk in there with open arms and ask for the key. My guess is Jordan came up with an elaborate scheme to avoid contact himself."

"Samantha was Rick's girl, right?" Smoke asked.

"Yeah," I answered.

"The Planner sent the gunman, correct?" Smoke put his hand under his chin, deep in thought.

"He did," I replied and looked out of the window, putting the information I gained to formulate a plan to keep us out of prison.

"Rick is the key," Smoke suggested. "The Planner needs Rick to swipe the plan because he can't do it himself. It would be a bad idea to contact Rick. So..."

I'd thought about what Smoke had said. He didn't have all the information I got from Samantha or the gunman. I'd sent him to guard the door when I questioned her, and then the gunman knocked him out. The info I'd gained I had yet to fill everyone on since leaving the hotel.

Smoke continued. "The Planner will need to remain lowkey throughout the heist, and Rick would have to appear normal for it to work."

"What are you getting at?" Bear asked. "Rick could let the police know what's up when he got there."

"Not if he didn't know Samanta was safe," Bruce added.

"I figured it out," Smoke muttered.

I looked at Smoke, intrigued about what he'd discovered.

Smoke continued, "We need to wait for Rick's vehicle to show up. It's perfect for what The Planner is trying to do. If Rick contacted you," he looked at me. "that means he didn't contact the FBI. The police don't have a clue what's going on. The Planner would want to keep it that way."

"We get there beforehand and stop Rick's car," I said. "That's how we save my mother."

"We need to figure out a way to get inside the impound," Smoke suggested.

"I have wire cutters in the back," I through out there. "we could cut through the fence and get set up before Jordan is there."

"Good," Smoke said. "we can use them."

"We need a disguise if anything," Bruce said. "we could pretend that we're working security for the impound. The Planner guy would never expect it."

"That's a good fucking idea," Smoke said.

Wha..., I thought. Smoke giving Bruce props for an idea? Bruce was turning out to be helpful like Kim thought. I guess Smoke was beginning to see that in him.

"Where are we gonna get uniforms our size at this time without ordering customs?" Bear asked as we approached a stop sign.

"We could pull up on some cops," Bruce said.

"Four of them," Smoke said sarcastically. "we'll get in a shootout, playboy."

"Damn," I said when an answer came to mind. "I didn't think about it until now. There are police uniforms under the seat. They belonged to the Africans. I remember seeing them when I searched the vehicle. I never mentioned anything about them because I thought they were useless. I counted three of them, leaving us one short."

"Shid," Smoke said. "We're in there then. Someone will stay back in case shit gets crazy. Not it."

Bear spoke up. "Not it."

"What the fuck," Bruce said, confused. "People still say that?"

"Hell yeah, nigga," Smoke told him. "and you're it."

"There's only one problem," I said.

"Oh shit," Smoke sighed. "you shoulda said something before I jumped out there. What is it?"

"The police badges say South African police, not American police," I informed them.

"That's it," Smoke said. "It's gonna be dark outside. We'll be good."

We came up with a general plan. Get there before Jordan dressed as policemen. Wait for Rick's car to enter the impound. From there, it's up in the air. I got no choice but to save my mother. There was one more thing I had to do before risking my life another time. I dialed Kim and told her what was going on in case I didn't make it home. This could be the last time I ever speak to her. Therefore, my last words to her were, "I love you."

Chapter 45: Rick

I felt my body lift from the ground. I was weak and disoriented after Adrian did a number on me. Lucky me, I was still breathing. I would say that I'm fortunate to be alive, but they weren't finished with me yet. I have to somehow stop Jordan and Adrian from hijacking an airplane. Mrs. Simmons was another story. I could get her out of this mess if she wants my help. It didn't seem like she did when I had the phone. I could have called the cops, and the rest would've been history. Kane lost his father, and I was trying my damndest to save his mother. The way she'd been acting, I don't know if that's possible.

"Is he up?" I heard Jordan's voice.

"He's coming around," Adrian's voice sounded to my right.

"Do something to get'em up," Jordan said.

I felt a hard slap across my face. "Sonofva," I groaned and grabbed the side of my jaw. "I'm up. You didn't have to slap me."

"Welcome back," Jordan said.

"Whatever, asshole," I said. I got a bit confident with my speech. Cherry was safe, so I had a little wiggle room to say what I want. I have to remind myself not to get too wild. I do want to live.

Jordan focused on me through the rearview mirror. "I know you didn't call the police."

"I called your mother," I joked, and that was a mistake. Adrian slapped me hard enough that it felt like he knocked all of my teeth loose. "Shit, I forgot you two are brothers."

"Got any more momma jokes?" I saw Jordan smile at me through the mirror.

I didn't answer. The best thing for me to do was keep my mouth shut. It was late, so I figured the police impound would be our next stop. I was beginning to regret coming after Jordan alone. I kind of miss having a partner, even if it was him.

"Now that I got your attention," Jordan turned onto the next street as he spoke. "I want to go over my new plan."

New plan, I thought.

"Since you feel like being brave," Jordan said. "poke your chest out and risk that whore's life. You won't have any problem going inside with Adrian. Noti will stay in the car with me, and we'll head to the plane yard and wait for you to arrive with the key for the fence."

"Your plan will fail," I said. "They'll recognize Adrian when he enters the front door."

Jordan smiled. "You forgot something, smart guy. No one will notice him. Adrian isn't wanted in America. Only you and I know about him. I wiped his information from the system over the years."

Dammit, that's right, I thought. I was stuck with Adrian. He was going to be a security dog, watching my every move. Getting out of the impound alive was going to be difficult with Adrian at my neck. It would be simpler if Mrs. Simmons went inside with me. From there, we could've had the protection to escape these monsters.

"You don't look excited," Jordan said and laughed.

I sucked my teeth and looked out of the window. I had to come up with a plan fast. We were about thirty minutes from the police impound. I felt Adrian's eyes on me, and I refused to look in his direction. Maybe he wanted me to feel scared. He posses the skill set of a deadly cobra, and I was his prey. Adrian is at the top of his class, and I was a new student. This was a lose-lose situation.

"I bet you're wondering why Noti jumped ship," I heard Jordan's voice.

He interrupted my train of thought. It was like Jordan want me to know he has the upper hand on me. Mrs. Simmons working with him was shocking, but I was intrigued about their relationship. What was on her mind when she decided Jordan was the answer? I turned my attention on Mrs. Simmons.

She had an angry look on her face. "We don't have to get into details." Her eyes were pinned on Jordan.

"Listen, princess," Jordan snapped. "you're not the only one here with something to lose. You thought you could use me to get what you want then bail without any consequences? Rick is a smart guy, even though I hate to admit it. He knows already. I guarantee it."

Mrs. Simmons looked and me with a concerned look. I tried to figure out what she had on her mind by her facial expression. I concluded she didn't want Kane to know she was working with the man who set up her son. The reaction I got from her outside the bar explained it clearly.

"Money," Jordan continued. "It's all about the benjamins. Jar ran an elaborate smuggling operation in African that extended around the world. He was the top guy in the business. I'm sure you were intelligent enough to figure out Jar was the king of a criminal empire. And guess who was his queen, helping build the most profound smuggling organization known to man?"

The information shocked me. Kane's mother helped Jar run his smuggling business. *How did I miss it?* I focused on bringing down Jordan and failed to see what was in front of my face. Jordan became the only person that mattered to me. Mrs. Simmons wasn't the innocent woman I first met at the office. She went silent, devastated by her husband's death. *Did she plan this while in Hill Heights? And what about Kane,* I thought. *Does he know about his mother?* Differents accusations swam around my mind, trying to piece together the details.

"Don't think about it so hard," Jordan interrupted. "it's bad for your health. If you want to find out more, stick with us."

"And become your crony," I said. "never."

Jordan laughed. "So you don't want to be a hero?"

"What the hell are you talking about?" I asked.

I saw a smile spread across his face in the mirror. "Africa. If we make it there without any issues, I'll let you see Jar's headquarters before I kill you. I'll anonymously report your dead body back to the American police. They'll find it, and your name will go down in history as the officer who discovered a massive smuggling base. That's the least I can do for you."

Jordan wants me to see the base of the operation. That would be his way of throwing it in my face. The asshole was being arrogant, but that would be his downfall. It could be a way to convince me to go along with hijacking the aircraft. Then kill me once were past American air portal. I began to consider helping them get the plane. If I could get to Africa alive, I could uncover the largest smuggling headquarters in the world. Opportunities like this just don't fall out of the sky into your lap. This would mean a lot for my career if I decided to take a risk. I sighed, thinking is it worth it?

Chapter 46: Kane

"How do I look?" Smoke asked after dressing in the African police uniform.

"Like you have experience," Bruce said sarcastically.

Bear chuckled, "Got'em"

Smoke eyed Bruce with a look on his face that said his remark wasn't funny. "Whatcha laughing about?" he turned his attention on Bear.

"Nigga it was funny," Bear replied.

"Focus," I told them.

Smoke sucked his teeth, "a'ight."

"Shirt a bit tight, but it's all good," Bear said and flexed his arms. The sleeves hugged his biceps and looked like they were about to pop.

"Don't ruin the shirt, pimp," I said while buttoning up the uniform. It was a perfect fit. I remembered what the General looked like. He was a huge man, built like a brick house, and no one in his army was of the same size. Thinking about the Africans brought back memories of my friend, Redd. Fuck, that shit hit me hard.

"Look at that," Smoke said, surprised. "My strap fits in the holster." He put on the police hat to complete the uniform.

"That shit looks funny as hell," Bear said. "you have way too much hair."

Smoke's dreads were thicker than mine, so I gave him my hat. "Try this one. It's bigger." I traded with him. I pinned my dreads back and put on the cap. It wasn't a perfect fit, but it worked.

"Much better," Smoke fitted the cap on his head. "right on."

"No problem," I put my gun in the holster and checked myself over. You would've thought we were with the African police if it wasn't for one thing.

"You guys look good except for the kicks," Bruce commented, looking down at our feet. "there aren't any dress shoes under the seat?"

"Hell nah," Smoke spoke up. "I'm not wearing any other shoes but my own. Nigga, have you seen what African feet look like?"

"Bruh," Bear said. "I used to date an African girl with a fat ass, but her dogs fuck everything up. I couldn't do it."

We laughed.

"Chill," I said. "all Africans don't have bad feet."

"Shid," Smoke replied. "name one who doesn't?"

"Miss South Africa," I answered.

"Her shit probably fucked up too," Smoke said.

I grabbed the wire cutters from the bed of the truck. "Ok, here's what we're gonna do." After going over the plan with my crew, we headed for the police impound. Bruce parked a safe distance from the location. Smoke and Bear hoped out with me. I turned to Bruce, "if shit gets crazy...bounce without us. You helped enough."

Bruce didn't answer right away. I could tell something was on his mind. "I won't hesitate."

I signed with a nod, and he did the same. I backed away from the vehicle and joined my crew.

"We good?" Smoke asked.

"Yeah," I said and led the way through a large field with tall grass. We got to a tall fence with bobwire at the top, preventing anyone from climbing over. I looked through to the other side and saw a graveyard full of police confiscated vehicles such as cars, trucks, boats, and airplanes. The landscape was massive.

"See anybody," I asked, scanning the area.

"Clear," Smoke said.

"Dry on my side," Bear said and got closer to the fence. "We're good."

"Alright," I began cutting open the fence. A few snips and we were in. I stepped through first. Smoke was second and then Bear.

"Fuck," Bear said. "I'm stuck."

I turned around and saw Bear caught in the fence by his shirt. "Don't move, or you'll rip it," I told him. I unhooked the piece of clothing.

"Damn," Bear said after he was free. "I fucked it up anyway."

I looked at the small rip on the side of his shirt. "It'll be fine. Let's move."

"Big goofy ass," Smoke muttered.

We were on the inside, covered by a row of cars. We moved to the next section without being detected. No security so far; the area was clear. A row of SUVs was ahead, and we made it safely across to them. I assumed we were the only ones in the yard. Who gonna break into a place like this at 8 pm besides a man who wanted to go to jail? *Oh, The Planner,* I thought.

"A'ight," I said as we settled between two SUVs. "you know what to do."

"Love," Smoke said.

"Love," I said, and we dapped hands.

I turned to Bear, and we dapped. "Love."

"Love," Bear repeated. "be safe."

It was our way of saying goodbye in case one of us didn't make it out alive. We have been friends for a long time, and after everything we had gone through together, how could we not love one another? I watched them run off in different directions. I sighed as they vanished into the night, thinking if I would ever see them again without being behind bars if we happened to get arrested. I shook the thought from my mind. "Tighten up, Kane." It wasn't the time to think negatively. I got my shit together and moved to the location I thought it would end. "Magnificant," I said, standing in front of a row of Learjets.

Chapter 47: Jordan

I saw the look on Rick's face. I had him where I wanted him. Surely he was contemplating what I'd said. Nothing pleased me more than to see him indecisive about the offer. He would be a hero, but that wouldn't mean much to him because he would be a dead hero. That would be his fate.

I continued driving down the road. We were minutes away from the police impound. *Time to get in the fucking zone.* What we were about to do could cost me everything I'd work for if things go wrong. I could've settled with killing Kane and getting back the money. That would've been much easier.

Why didn't I take that route instead, I thought.

The Planner's burning desire for a fucking thrill put me in this situation. He was taking control of my mind every second of the day he became more toxic. There was close to nothing left of Jordan. The only piece of life Jordan had left sat in the backseat.

"Remember, once we're inside, my plane is the Learjet 24," Adrian told Rick. "It's the only 24 on the lot. After we get the key for the fence, we'll be clear to fly."

"Learjet 24, huh," Rick scoffed. "I'm in the wrong line of work."

"We had five of them," Noti commented.

"Use for transporting weapons?" Rick asked.

"No," Notie told him. "We used them to transport money."

"Can you fly?" Rick continued.

"No," she said. "if I could, you wouldn't be here."

I smiled, Noti was vicious, but I'm glad she mentioned the planes. I'd already put together how I would take my share and run. At least one aircraft had to be in flight condition. That would be my ticket off the continent. I drove another thirty seconds and noticed something peculiar up ahead. I turned my head towards a black Humvee as we passed by it.

What the hell...

It resembled the same make and model as the African drove. I couldn't see inside beyond the dark tinted windows. *Fuck,* I thought. *Are the Africans on to me? They couldn't be.* And then it hit me. Kane drove away that day in the Hummer with my money. *Could it be him?* Something about that didn't sit right with me. Maybe I was just paranoid. The Africans fucked up my mind every since that day. They want to kill me for what happened at the warehouse. The General didn't get what he wanted, and that meant death. There could be a chance they never left America and were waiting for me to lead them to the diamond. *Rick...he used the phone to call the General? Why would Rick work with those savages?* He could've been pressured and left without an option. I had to get focused on the task. No way was I gonna turn back now.

The police impound was in range. I stopped the car a good distance from the entrance and got out. "Noti, you're with me." I pulled out my gun and made sure it was loaded. "We'll meet you at the plane site," I told Adrian.

"What is it?" Adrian asked.

"Someone is on to us," I told him. "The Humvee we passed belongs to the Africans. The truck was reinforced with military-grade armor, and it's bulletproof. There's only two in the world that were specially designed to protect the General." I paused and looked at Notie. "And her son has one of them."

Chapter 48: Rick

"And her son has one of them," Jordan told Adrian.

I watched Jordan and Mrs. Simmons jog off in the opposite direction, heading towards the Humvee. I exhaled, thinking about what Jordan would do to Kane if he got ahold of him. Mrs. Simmons would be there to watch her son die, and Jordan would give a monkey's ass. I thought the Hummer looked familiar when we first passed by it. The truck belonged to the Africans. Jordan confirmed it. I remembered seeing the vehicle at the warehouse after Jordan mentioned it. Now that I think about it, Kane did drive off in one. *Dammit,* I thought. The kid is in trouble, and there wasn't anything I could do about it.

Adrian pushed me out of the car. "Drive," he got into the front seat.

I don't know why but I strapped on my seatbelt. It wasn't like I was going to be driving anywhere far. The police impound was directly in front of us. It could have something to do with Adrian. The man carried a demeanor that could scar a lion.

I put the car in drive and pulled forward until we reached the front gate. I noticed one security guard. He was waiting inside the security booth watching TV. I didn't want to give the officer a chance to interact with Adrian, so I immediately flashed my FBI badge. I rolled down the window. "FBI, we're here to investigate a Learjet 24 that was confiscated a few weeks ago."

"FBI," the security stood and stepped closer to the car. He looked over my badge. "Didn't you guys search that plan yesterday?"

"Yeah," I said. "but the Director wasn't satisfied with the evidence gathered from the search, so he sent us out to perform a more thorough check."

He bent low and looked in the vehicle at Adrian. "A more thorough check, huh. Well, then...I just need to inform my boss you guys are back, and then you'll be good to go."

"No need," I said. "I spoke with him before we arrived. He knows we're here."

He looked at us skeptically. "That's weird because he called out sick today." He backed away from the vehicle, and before I could react. Adrian's arm reached across my face. He was fast, unlike anyone I'd ever witnessed in my life. I turned in the direction of the security guard. He was sprawled out on the ground with a dagger in his neck. He gasped for air and reached for his throat. Blood began to pour from his mouth, and he choked to death.

Adrian got out of the car and retrieved his dagger. He walked inside the booth, and I heard a loud sound in front of us. He dragged the officer into the booth and propped the body in the seat as if the guard was still watching TV. He then got back inside of the car. "Drive."

I drove through the gate as Adrian ordered me to do. He murdered an officer in cold blood in front of my eyes. I wanted to rip out his throat. *Why didn't I do anything to help? Protect and serve,* I thought. That's the code every officer lives by. I want to feel like I was doing the right thing. An innocent man died, and it wouldn't be the last. I looked at Black Water from the corner of my eyes. His face was emotionless. The sonofvabitch didn't show any remorse for what he'd done. As an officer of the law, I felt ashamed for not living by the code.

We came to the main office. I stopped the car on the side of the building, avoiding the front to prevent anyone from seeing Adrian. The last thing I wanted was to allow him to slay someone else. I prepared to get out of the car and walk inside. That never happened. I spotted an officer walking from the other side of the lot. This guy was huge. It looked like he belonged in the NFL. He stopped in front of the car and looked at us through the windshield. "Field security," I told Adrian. "I'll handle it."

"Don't take too long," Adrian had his dagger ready for another kill.

"I can get the key for the fence without you killing anyone else," I didn't look at him when I spoke. My door was opened and shut before he could respond. I walked to the front of the car and met the officer.

"Officer," the huge man said.

"I need the key for the plane yard fence?" I asked. A confused expression shaped his face. Something was off about this guy, starting with his uniform. The side of his shirt was ripped, and he had on Air Jordan tennis shoes. I never looked down at them. They could've been Shaqs by the size of his feet. The uniform colors were slightly off like he'd washed it too many times, but that wasn't the case. I was the best profiler in the department, and it was clear to me this guy was a fraud.

"It's open," he pointed in the direction of the plane yard. His arm muscles were the size of my head. He was definitely an intimidating guy.

Open, I thought. "Ok," I didn't want to carry the conversation any longer than I to. He shifted a bit due to the headlights beaming from the car. I got a good look at his face before the badge on his shirt reflected the light back into my eyes. He looked just like the kid who speared me two years ago at Kane's school. It had to be him, and that meant Kane was somewhere close. Jordan was right about the Humvee. I backed off and got back into the vehicle.

"The key," Adrian kept his eyes on the kid.

"It's open," I informed him. Hopefully, Black Water didn't notice the kid pretending to be a security guard. I put the car in drive, thinking about the predicament and what I read on the kid's badge. *South African Police,* I thought and continued to the plane yard. I put my foot on the gas pedal, and the car didn't move. The vehicle revved as I felt a rise in position. *What the hell?* I looked through the rearview mirror and couldn't believe what I saw. The kid had lifted the vehicle off the ground by the bumper. He looked like Lou Ferrigno in the 1977 movie, The Incredible Hulk. It was stunning to behold such extraordinary strength. The car dropped and accelerated forward. I stomped on the brakes, stopping the car a few feet ahead. The passenger seat was empty. Adrian had vanished.

I heard a commotion behind the car. Adrian and the kid were face to face, sizing each other up. I got out to help. I couldn't let the kid die. "Adrian," I tried to distract him by shouting his name, and it didn't bother him at all. The dagger flew from his hand and struck the kid in the chest. He had moved out of the way in the nick of time.

"Ah," the kid roared like a wild beast. He grabbed his chest and removed the blade in one pull. Blood soaked the spot on his shirt where the dragger struck.

It was the first time Adrian had failed to kill with his primary weapon. The kid held the dagger in his hand. Adrian had given him a weapon. The kid, Adrian, and I were standing in a circle facing one another, waiting for someone to move. By now, Adrian had to know I was on the kid's side.

"We have to attack together," I told the kid. It was the only way we would win.

The kid nodded and made the first move. He attacked with the dagger. Adrian maneuvered from harm's way and countered with a kick to his gut. I took the opportunity to attack and threw a punch while Adrian was distracted. He swiftly blocked my shot, and I caught a roundhouse kick to the face, followed by a defensive leg sweep that put me on my back. His foot came down on my chest as Bruce Lee had performed in Enter the Dragon. I clenched up in a ball with my arms around my chest. Pain shot through my body from the powerful blow.

"Ah..." I heard the kid in the background and reluctantly opened my eyes to see what was going on.

The kid rushed Adrian and wrestled him onto the ground. He balled his fists together and hammered Adrian's face. I rolled to the side, still in pain, witnessing the unexpected rage the kid possessed. I got up, stumbled down to a knee, and spat out blood. Adrian tried to block the kid's blows, but he was too strong. I figured he outweighed Adrian by at least one hundred pounds. He continued to pummel Adrian like an angry gorilla on a chimpanzee. Suddenly, the kid got on his feet and lifted Adrian off the ground. Adrian pouched the kid in the head out of desperation, but it didn't faze him. I watched the kid throw Adrian against the side of the building, and he bounced off the structure then fell to the ground. When Adrian didn't move, I'd thought the kid won. *He did it,* I thought.

"Where's Kane?" I asked the kid, and I wish I hadn't. The kid looked at me, and that was enough time for Adrian to regain consciousness. He rushed the kid and landed a flying kick. The kid fell to the ground and instantly produced a gun. Adrian kicked it from his hand, and surprisingly, it slid over to me. I grabbed the weapon, aimed, and fired multiple shots. "Fuck," I muttered. Adrian had disappeared into the night.

Chapter 49: Jordan

The Humvee came into view. I stopped a short distance away from the vehicle on the opposite side of the street. Noti was at my side with a worried look on her face. We moved at a normal walking speed. "Wipe that worried look off of your face," I told her. "This isn't the first time your son and I had a conflict. He's smarter than you think."

"I'm not worried about my son," she replied. "I'm worried about you."

I stopped in my tracks, looked at her, and grinned. "And why is that?"

"If my son kills you," she said. "I won't get what I want."

"What makes you think that will happen?" I asked while keeping my eyes on the hummer.

"Because nothing will stop him from bringing me home safely." She said.

"What if I kill him?" I looked her in the eyes, taking my attention off the vehicle.

"A caring mother would never let that happen," she stared fearlessly into my eyes, giving me the impression she would push past any limitation to protect her child.

"We'll see," I continued walking just past the vehicle. It was killing me that I couldn't get a clean look inside. Regardless, somebody's day was about to get a whole lot worse. Noti stayed close behind when I crept up to the truck. I approached the side cautiously without being detected. It would've been easier if I didn't have this bitch beside me. On the bright side of things, she could watch her son die by my hands. I couldn't wait to see the look on her face when he stops breathing his last breath.

Knock, knock, I said in my mind as I tapped on the driver's side window. My gun was out and ready to catch a body. I immediately checked the door handle. *Unlocked. Lucky me.* It wasn't Kane or even the Africans here to chop off my fucking head. Instead, an enormous motherfucker stepped out of the vehicle with his hands up.

"Take it easy," he said with a straight face. "I don't have anything for you."

"Where is Kane?" I asked. "And who the fuck are you?"

He studied me for about ten seconds. "Kane who?"

"Don't fuck with me," I told him. "where is he?" I held the gun up to his head.

"I told you," he lowered his hands. "I don't have-"

Lowering his hands was the first mistake. I hit him on the side of his head with the butt of my weapon. "One more time, tough guy." I was surprised when he didn't fall. His face turned to the side. A small amount of blood trickled down his face.

"Look, man," he faced forward and looked square in my eyes. "you can take the truck if that's what you want. I don't know who you're talkin' about."

"You're fault," This kid had to of gone insane to value Kane's life over his own. "time to die."

"No," Noti stepped in front of the gun.

"What the fuck are you doing?" I tried to shove her out of the way.

"You're letting your emotions get the best of you," she said. "police are all over the place. Did you forget we're by a government impound?"

I sighed. Fuck, Noti was right. If I dropped this kid, the police would hear the gunfire, and my plan would be blown to shit. Officers would respond in minutes. I stood there thoughtless, trying to figure out what to do with this big ass kid, and that was a mistake.

I didn't see him coming, and I caught the most vicious right hook under my chin. What the hell was I thinking by letting my guard down? The shot was powerful, and the force behind it propelled me into the air. It was an awkward momentum that sent my body sideways, and I bounced off the side door then hit hard on the ground. He had stepped around Noti using the bob and weave attack like Iron Mike did his opponents in the ring. The tactic was genius. "Fuck," I muttered. No one throughout my entire life hit me that hard. I touched my chin to make sure it was still attached to my head. I didn't think about the gun I'd lost hold of after the punch. Wondering if I would ever be able to speak again without drooling was a more significant concern.

"Get up," I heard a voice from above, and it wasn't God's.

He threw me against the truck and began pounding on me like a punching bag. Blow after blow sent an excruciating amount of pain in my chest. This kid was fucking my world up to the extent that made me want to die, and it seemed like it would never end. The worst was yet to come. He grabbed my whole head with his massive mitts. His hands were large enough to wrap around my entire head. Then I felt the bulletproof window collide with the front of my face. *What the fuck is this kid doing to me?* Over and over again, I felt my head slam against the glass. The only way he would stop was if the glass shattered, and that wouldn't happen.

"Like that?" He taunted confidently.

He released his hold, and I slowly slid down the vehicle. My legs reluctantly gave out, and they buckled under my weight. I couldn't keep my eyes open as my vision faded in and out. Nothing was in view. Everything in sight was blurry, like an unfocused camera lens. *Where are my glasses?* And then I remembered having 20/20 vision. Disorient and confusion came over me about who I was and where I was. I could've sworn I was with my little brother Adrian. Why wasn't he trying to help stop this monster?

"Stop it," I heard a women's voice. "he's had enough."

Was I on a date? I got my ass kicked in front of my woman, I thought. The attack ceased, and somehow I was standing on my feet. It was like I was floating or, better yet, hovering just above the ground. The collar of my shirt tightened, and then I understood someone was holding me up. My head swirled around my neck in a circle, and I said. "You had enough...tough guy?" why would I say that when I was definitely losing the fight. That's what I was doing, right? I couldn't remember anymore.

"Release him now," I heard my girlfriend in the background, and I couldn't believe she wasn't jumping in to help either.

My body dropped down like a melting popsicle on a hot summer day. I shook my head rapidly from side to side, groggily. The only thing I felt like during was lying down in my bed. I gain some strength in my legs. It wasn't much but enough to get the hell up. I stumbled around, dazed, and fell against the truck. I was so scared I started swinging at the air until I hit my target. "Damnit," that wasn't it. I'd punched the truck. Nobody was in front of me when I unsteadily fell back from the vehicle. "Fuck," I spat out and walked off in a drunken state.

"Where are you going?" I heard my girlfriend.

"Home," I said back to her.

"You're walking in the wrong direction," she said.

Honestly, I didn't know which way was home. I turned around and stood there, looking like an idiot. "Which way to the house, honey?" I pointed in every direction.

"You," she aimed a gun at the man who assaulted me. "help him get in the backseat."

"Hey," I pointed at her. "where did you get a gun?" The big guy walked over and grabbed my shoulder. "Don't touch my asshole. I meant you, asshole." I shrugged my arm away in a frustrated manner. "I can help myself." My woman held the guy at gunpoint as I opened the back door. "Why didn't you...use that thing when I was getting my ass...my ass kicked?" I watched her head shake at me, and I waved her off then got inside the truck. I laid down across the seat. It felt extremely confrontable, and I wanted to close my eyes.

I heard the vehicle doors open and shut.

"You know you can go to jail for assaulting a police officer?" I told the man who was now seated in the passenger seat. "Tell'em, honey? Your ass is going to prison for a long time, tough guy." I held my ribs. They ached, and I was short of breath. "I work for the FBI. I bet you...didn't know that." I continued talking smack. It was the only thing I could do.

"Shut up," I heard my woman. "you don't work for anybody."

"One more thing, honey?" I asked. "I need to go to the hospital."

Boom!

I heard a shot ring out, and my reflexes ordered me to flinch. I felt all over my chest and head. I didn't get shot, and I reluctantly sat up to see who had. It was my job as an officer.

"Drive through the front gate up ahead," my boo told the man. She still had the gun aimed at him.

The truck began to move, and we drove up to a large area with a gate. I read the sign off to the side in big red letters. "Police impound," I muttered. "What the hell are we doing here?"

"Just shut up," she told me.

"Why are you so rude today," I asked. "can't you see I'm hurt?" I noticed a body of some sort sprawled out on the ground. "Shit, he looks dead. Stop the vehicle, so I can check on him? We need to inform the police."

"Keep driving through the gate," she ordered him, and he drove right past the body.

"What are you doing?" I said hysterically. "That was an officer!"

"Shut your mouth," she snapped at me. "you're not an agent." She faced forward and said. "There they are. Drive straight through the fence ahead."

"What's going on?" I asked. Who was she talking about? *They...they who?* I was about to find out, seconds later, we crash through the fence. I saw a spark in the front of the vehicle as we broke the lock into a yard full of air plans. The vehicle slid to a stop. I couldn't believe what I was seeing. My brother Adrian was holding down a kid at gunpoint.

Chapter 50: Kane

I cut through the fence with the wire cutters and entered the area with the planes. I have to admit they are beautiful. I'd never seen one this close before. The jets came in different shapes, sizes, and colors. *Are these the type of planes my father used to travel in?* I didn't have the slightest idea of how much one would cost, but all of them looked expensive. Which one belonged to Jordan was what I had to figure out. If I post by the correct plane, I could catch Jordan before he could escape. The yard was enormous, and I was having a difficult time choosing one. There was only one method I knew that worked every time.

Any mini, miny moe, catch a tiger by his toe…

My finger stopped on a black and red plane with gold trim. I got closer to the aircraft and looked it over, thinking if there was a way I could get inside. The door didn't appear to have a keyhole by the handle. *Ok,* I thought that was odd. I pulled the handle, and the door lifted open with ease. The inside of the plane smelt new. I scanned around the inside of the aircraft. There were four seats and a section where the pilot could store cargo in the back. I stepped in and moved to the cockpit. The dashboard was covered with buttons, switches, gauges, and three screens. A steering wheel was station in front of both front seats—one for the pilot and co-pilot. *Wow,* the system seemed complex.

I thought about hiding somewhere inside of the plane. Then changed my mind. If I chose the wrong one, Jordan could getaway and take my mother with him. I didn't want that to happen, so I came up with another idea. I could trash the plane, make it unflyable. That wasn't a bright idea either. There were several planes and not enough time to ruin them all. And...someone could hear. I had a decision to make. I thought about what to do as I sat in the front seat on the right. I sighed and relaxed in the chair. It was comfortable. If I weren't here to save my mother, I would have fallen asleep in it. I did lay my head back, and I saw something I didn't notice before. There were a few more buttons and switches across a top panel. There was one button in particular that grabbed my attention. "Engine start," I said to myself.

I wondered if I pushed the button would it start. I searched for an ignition keyhole, but I didn't see one. I looked at the central dashboard between the seats. There was a clutch for pilots to trust the plane into the air, but no key start. Maybe you didn't need a key to turn on the engine? I had everything in front of me: an engine start button, pedals, and a steering wheel. I bet you could drive this machine like a car? Right then, I came up with an idea. I looked up at the engine start button. I wasn't planning on flying anywhere but if I could start the plane. Maybe that would be enough to put some fear in Jordan's heart. He wouldn't try to steal an aircraft with an officer in the yard, would he? He wouldn't have to see me…just hear the plane.

I reached for the button. It was like I was moving in slow motion. Just before I was about to press it, I heard gunfire. "Wha…" I pulled my finger back and looked through the front window. I didn't see anybody at that exact moment. "Shit," I had no way to contact Smoke or Bear. We'd turned off our phones and hid them under the seat. I continued looking through the window, searching for The Planner. He was here. That was the only reason for gunfire. I continued listening, but no other shots were fired. A shootout should have erupted after the first shot. That's how it went any other time we got in an altercation. Unless…it only took one bullet? I wanted to check on my boy, but I knew I couldn't move. The night sky covered the area. It was completely dark outside, and nothing could be seen far off in the distance. Sitting there waiting for someone to appear was intense and caused a sense of paranoia. It was how I felt when I was in the backseat with Ke'Mo Cutt.

"You must be Kane," someone took me by surprise.

I turned around with a sense of urgency. How did I miss this guy? He stood around six feet, and by the expression on his face, I could tell meant business. I didn't see a gun in his hands, and if he had one, it would've been in my face. That meant he wasn't the person who fired the shot. "Who are you?" I noticed someone had put a beatdown on his face. He had fresh bruises and a busted lip. I wanted to asked who fucked him up like that.

The guy didn't answer as he carefully stepped inside of the plane.

I held my guard and pulled out my weapon before he got any closer. I had my run in's with psychopaths dealing with Jordan, and this time I wanted to start with the advantage. He stopped, and we stood face to face. "I asked, who are you? Don't answer if you want your shit pushed back."

"The owner of this plane, kid," he said with his hands down by his side.

"Jordan's brother," I asked. "and put your fuckin' hands up so I can see them." He began to move. "Slowly."

He slowly put his hands up as I'd ask. "Brother is a strong word. Jordan is more of an acquaintance."

"Get the fuck out here," I said. "He's your brother. Who fired the shot?"

He smirked at me and shrugged. "Don't know."

"Bullshit," I growled. "don't test me."

"A cop," he said. "we're at a police impound. I expected better security. Not some kid pretending to be an officer with an African police badge. Same uniform as the big guy I dealt with earlier."

Bear, I thought. *This guy ran into him. Bear did that to his face.* "Did you kill my friend?" I was so mad the gun was shaking in my hand. I had an itch to blow his head off.

The smirk on his face was replaced with a more serious expression. "You're nervous."

"Shut the fuck up," I said sternly. There was a possibility he killed Bear. My mind began putting clues together. The gunfire and this guy, showing up with a busted face. "Where is Jordan and my mother? I know they're with you." I had to focus. If he took out Bear, then he's dangerous. Bear could rip a man to shreds. And this guy was standing here without Bear on his ass. Then...I shook the thought from my mind.

"You ask a lot of questions," he said.

"Where is my mo-" I'd got too close and paid for it. The guy did some Jackie Chan shit and took the gun away, then hit me in the face. I ate the punch but couldn't do anything about the gun, so I rushed him before he could shoot.

We landed in the back cargo area. The space wasn't big enough for both of us to be wrestling around. I landed on top, taking advantage. He pointed the gun in my face, and I moved to the side and grabbed his hand. He had a firm grip and was determined not to let go of it. Finally, I pried it from him. "Ah..." I fell off him after taking a punch to my lower abdominal where I was slit open by Abel. The wound still hurts like hell. We stood up at the same time. I couldn't let him win, so I blocked out the pain I felt in my stomach. I had the weapon, but he was fast enough to kick it away and follow up with another kick to my head, then chest. I was sent flying into the cockpit and fell against the controls. He was swift...fast as lightning. He didn't need a gun to defeat me. I instantly realized his superior combat skills. This was one of those guys you saw in a kung fu movie. You would think it was the producer editing the film to make him appear faster than he was. Nah, this guy was the real deal.

He wiped blood away from the side of his mouth with his thumb. "What the hell are they feeding kids these days?" His words were sarcastic.

I regained my balance as he rushed me. Suddenly, he launched into the air and tried to fly-kick me. I maneuvered to the side in the cramped space, and he kicked the dashboard. But he wasn't done. Even though I dodge his attack, he countered with an elbow to my face. I reached out in a desperate attempt to grab him and was successful. He was trapped in a bearhug, and I tried to squeeze hard enough that the pressure would cause his head to explode. For a moment, it had work.

"Ah..." he cried out as I crushed him in my arms. Somehow he had enough room to knee me multiple times in my gut.

I held onto him anyway, fighting off the pain and trying to strategize my next move. He might have the skills, but I was bigger and stronger. The gut shots became more aggressive. He was a mouse struggling to stay alive in a snake's hold. My hands were in use, and there wasn't enough space to counter with a knee shot of my own. I thought about what my father would tell me in a challenging situation.

Use your head, son.

That's what he would say, and that's what I did. I gave Jordan's brother the meanest fuckin' headbutt he's ever felt.

"…" he had a muffled cry, and the knee shots stopped.

The powerful blow dazed me as well but was more effective against him. I felt him lose a bit of life. The fight he once had diminished as I attacked him again. The second strike drained everything he had left. He felt lifeless in my arms as he passed out. I kept him locked in a bearhug for a few seconds longer just to make sure I finished him. He slumped under my hold like a baby who'd fallen asleep in their mother's arms. I let go after putting him in the left side seat. His eyes were closed, and there was no movement in his body. I sighed and fell back, exhausted. "What the fuck." I muttered.

"Kane," I heard someone call my name.

I jumped up like a paranoid drug dealer looking out for the cops. "Smoke…damn, dawg. You scared the hell out of me.

Smoke walked over to me. "Who the fuck is he?"

"Jordan's brother," I told him. I looked at his body, resting helplessly in the seat. I felt like punching him in the fuckin' face. Lucky for him, I'm not an asshole.

"You fuck his shit up," he said. He had his gun out and put it away in the holster. He slapped Jordan's brother on the face twice. "He's out cold."

"Yeah," I tried to move, but the pain in my abdomen forced me to bend over. I held the wound, figuring if I applied pressure, it would ease the pain. Shit didn't work.

"Seem like he fucked your shit up too," Smoke grabbed my shoulders and supported my weight by wrapping my arm around his neck. "Let's get the fuck outta here. Where is Bear?"

Smoke cautiously helped me off the plane. We were standing in the open. "I'ma be honest with you. I think he slumped Bear."

"Wha..." he said in shock. "Why didn't you put a bullet in that nigga head? Fuck that. I'll handle it."

"Ease up," I told him. "We gotta wait. If Jordan dipped, we'll need him to find my mother. Plus, we haven't confirmed if our boy is gone. He didn't say exactly."

"I can go with that," Smoke said. "I searched half the yard and didn't see any guards. We're straight for now, but we don't have much time before the police arrive. And if we're short on time, so is Jordan. I came runnin' because I heard a shot pop off. I thought it was going down."

"Well, I appreciate it," I sucked up the pain and straightened up on my won. "I gotta from here. Thanks for your help, my guy." I winced from the pain, but I was all right.

"Watch out!" Smoke shoved me to the ground.

Boom, boom!

I heard shots fired. Smoke fell onto the ground next to me.

"Ah..." Smoke reached for his leg.

I saw Jordan's brother standing in the doorway of the plan. "Fuck," he jumped out and ran in our direction. We had walked a reasonable distance away from the aircraft. Smoke would've gotten killed if we'd been any closer.

Smoke looked at me, "Take the gun," he slid it over to me. "I'm cool."

When Smoke first arrived on the plane. The gun slip from my mind because I was in so much pain. I'd left it on the aircraft, and that mistake got my best friend shot. I picked up the gun and fired. He stopped and took cover behind another plane. I grabbed under Smoke's shoulder with one hand and kept aim with the other as I dragged him to safety behind an enormous dark grey aircraft. It was the largest vehicle in the yard. "Wait here," I said.

"Kane," Smoke grabbed my arm before I could leave. "Don't kill 'em," he groaned in pain. "We still need him to find mom."

I nodded. "I'll be back." I gave him some dap and went on the attack. Jordan's brother could be anywhere, so I crept around the plane with caution. I made it three planes down, and there was still no sign of him anywhere. "Fuck!" I fell to the ground after being kicked from above. It was a great sneak attack that I ultimately didn't expect. I should've known he would hide on the wing of a plane. I was busy searching for him on the ground level. I'd dropped the gun, and it slid just out of arm's reach. I turned around to a gun in my face.

This was where my story would end. Everything that I had been through was for nothing, and I wouldn't take it back. Fuck it. I was ready to die. It was the life I chose the day I sat on the couch watching a few bank robbers shake the police with seventy grand.

I closed my eyes, prepared for death. I heard a loud sound that wasn't a bullet entering my skull. I immediately opened my eyes and saw the Humvee crash through the plane yard fence. The vehicle skidded to a stop about twenty yards away. The commotion grabbed the gunman's attention, also saving my life in the process. I picked up the gun and stood in time for a face-to-face showdown.

Chapter 51: Rick

"Sonofvabitch got away," I muttered as I looked around for Adrian. I slowly moved in the direction of the kid while keeping up my guard. "Are you ok?"

The kid sat up and sighed. "I had him," he stood and looked around the area.

"He's gone," I said. "and you don't want to go looking for a guy like him." The kid held his own against Black Water, and if it weren't for me, maybe he would've won the fight.

"Rick, right?" The kid asked.

"How do you know my name?" I replied.

"I'm Kane's friend," he said and dusted off dirt from his clothes.

"Of course," I began. "why didn't you tell him not to come here? Jordan and Adrian are highly wanted criminals. He should've informed the FBI as I asked him to do."

"What happened the last time he informed the FBI," he looked at me with a sarcastic expression.

"What are you talking about?" I said, confused.

"The warehouse," he looked me up and down like he wanted to knock my lights out. "yeah...that's what I thought. Y'all fucked that up and missed him. Now Kane's mother is in danger."

The kid was right. We screwed up, and Jordan escaped us. "That doesn't give you a reason to act on your own. This situation is still an FBI matter."

"Whatever whiteboy," he waved me off. "I just saved your ass. The FBI isn't coming to help. We're all you got. That guy Adrian is heading in that direction." He pointed to the plane yard. "Kane is waiting there for Jordan to show. I gotta go." He began to walk off.

"Wait a sec," I asked. "Kane is waiting for Jordan?"

"Yeah," he turned around. "And if I don't get there in time. It could turn out bad."

"Dammit," I muttered and looked toward the plane yard. "Ok, we should go help Kane, but before we leave, I have to let you know something in case I don't make it out alive."

"Speak," he said.

"Mrs. Simmons is not in danger like you think," his face turned up. "Jordan and Adrian are working for her. She's using them to get to Africa, where her husband's safehouse is located. Supposedly, there is a ton of money and supplies stashed at the headquarters."

The kid searched his mind for an answer. "I don't believe you."

"Believe what you want, kid," I told him. "I figured Kane needs to know the truth if things go sideways. I'm the only one who knows about their deal. We can still get Mrs. Simmons out of this without the feds finding out about her involvement."

"Why would you do that for her?" He asked.

"Because I know she's a good person, and so is Kane," I said. "I only want to catch Jordan and his brother. Kane's family has been through enough. And…I owe Kane two years of his life."

"What are you talking about?"

"I was with Jordan the day Kane got arrested at school," I said. "He served two years for a murder he didn't commit. Jordan took it to heart after Kane was found not guilty. He used Kane to get the diamond we were supposed to guard for federal purposes. His mother's breakdown after her husband's death affected her mentally. She needs help…not a jail cell. I also know…Abel murdered their father." After we investigated Abel, his fight with Kane, and Mrs. Simmons disowning him, it was easy to put together that Abel was the one who committed the murder.

The kid smirked. He turned from me and looked at the plane yard. "Alright then…let's go."

I sighed, wondering if he believed me or not. It didn't matter because he would still relay my message to Kane. That's what was important. I followed behind the kid, heading in the direction of the plane yard. Suddenly, I heard the sound of a motor roaring behind us. I turned around, and so did the kid. We both swiftly moved to the side as the Humvee I saw earlier came speeding by. The vehicle crashed through the fence that blocked off the runway for the planes. The kid and I gave each other a look that said things were about to get hot.

Chapter 52: Kane

I kept the gun on Jordan's brother as I surveyed the Humvee. Big Bruce must've known we were in trouble and came to help. I thought that he would've high-tailed it out of here by now. I could tell he was going through something emotionally when he first told me about T-Mac. I saw a sincere expression on his face. He doesn't want to be in this world alone. My house was the first place he came looking for a friend, and he didn't abandon us.

"I don't want to kill you, kid," he said. "I could've shot your friend in the head, but I spared his life. The only reason you're alive is because of your mother."

"What the fuck you talkin' about," I stepped closer to him right when the Humvee doors opened.

"Looks like you're about to find out," he stepped to the side.

I couldn't believe my eyes when Bruce, Jordan, and my mother stepped out of the vehicle. She had a gun in her hands. The first thing I thought was Bruce saved my mother from Jordan. I would soon find out I was wrong.

Jordan came running over. "Adrian," he shouted. "What the fuck are you doing? He's a kid."

Adrian? I thought it was strange that Jordan would try to stop his brother from killing me. I kept the gun on Adrian anyway. I couldn't trust The Planner.

"You sound like a cop," Adrian looked at Jordan as he approached.

"That's because I am," Jordan looked at me. "Are you alright, kid?"

I shifted the gun off Adrian to Jordan. I noticed a concerned look on his face. "You can stop the act." Jordan wanted me dead more than anybody, so why was he pretending like he cared if I died or not?

"It's not an act and drop your weapon," Jordan said. "my brother is a very dangerous man." He turned to him. "Adrian put the gun away, now."

"You must've hit your head," Adrian smirked. "What's wrong with him?"

He wasn't talking to me…he was speaking to my mother.

"The big guy slammed his head against the truck multiple times," my mother answered. "I would assume he has a severe head injury of some kind."

"Honey," Jordan turned to her. "You need to get back in the truck. It's too dangerous."

"And he thinks we're in a relationship," she sighed.

"Perfect," Adrian shook his head.

"Mother," I looked at her. "why are you talking like you know them? Jordan has been trying to kill me and took you from the hospital." I was utterly lost and taken off guard by what had transpired. Big Bruce had beaten Jordan to the point that he thinks he's an agent again. And he called my mother honey. The only thing I can't explain was why mother seemed calm around two dangerous men who kidnapped her.

"I'll explain everything later," she said. "right now…you have to get out of here."

"Wha…" that took me by surprise. She wanted me to leave without her. "I will never leave you with them." Adrian moved, and I shifted the gun on him.

"Kane," she cried. "listen to me…go, son. I love you."

"The best thing for you to do is listen to your mother," Adrian spoke up, and he was confident enough to lower his gun.

"It's the right thing to do, kid," Jordan said. "I can handle Adrian from here. He won't hurt-"

Adrian slapped Jordan over the head with his weapon. He turned the gun on Bruce. "Help me get him in the plane over there, and you both are free to go."

Bruce looked at me, and I signed for him to help. "My mother isn't going anywhere. She's coming with us."

"That's up to her, kid." Adrian stopped Bruce. "I wasn't talking about you. I was talking about him."

Rick. I didn't notice him and Bear were both approaching us. I wanted to be excited because my friend was still alive, but I couldn't. Everything was happening fast. My emotions were all over the place.

Rick had a gun in his hands and aimed at Adrian. "Are you sure you're not gonna try to kill me?"

"I have no hard feelings about earlier," Adrian told him.

"Rick," I said, even more confused by what was taking place. I had a gun, my mother had a gun, and so did he. We had the advantage, and nobody was taking action. "Shoot him."

"Kane," he said thoughtfully. "I can't do that." Rick began to help Adrian with Jordan.

"You're on their side?" I asked.

"I'm on your side," he said. "and always will be. You should have done what I asked. You have to get out of here before the police arrive."

Rick began helping Adrian with Jordan. My mother walked over and grabbed me by the face with both hands.

"You're like your father," she said and lowered my head to kiss my forehead. "I'll be ok. You need to leave now."

"Why," I asked emotionally. "I'm right here...we can leave together."

"You wouldn't understand," she told me with a tear streaming down her cheek. "I have to go with them."

I looked her in the eyes. The world stopped around me, and it was just us standing there alone. I felt my eyes get watery. I couldn't understand why she wanted to go. This should have ended. I had her back alive, and still...she felt distant. She was slowly breaking my heart, and I didn't know why she was doing this to me: her son...her own flesh and blood. My soul ached ten times worse than it ever had before. I felt like she was abandoning me to be with them, like a child left by their mother on someone's doorstep to be raised by a stranger. Piece by piece...my heart melted away.

"Take care of yourself," those were her last words before a rocket came humming in and exploded one of the planes.

Chapter 53: Kim

"I love you too," I hung up the phone with Kane. I knew what I had to do...I had to save my man. I couldn't let anything happen to him. He was going after The Planner. The last time Kane faced him, Redd was murdered in the process. I saw in his eyes how it affected him emotionally. His friend was gone, and there was no way to bring him back. I don't want to feel that way ever. To be left alone without Kane would be unbearable.

I didn't have much time before Kane would reach the police impound. I had to move fast. The gunman who was sent after Samantha could've killed him and Smoke. That was enough of a cause for me to worry. The Planner became a problem when we decided to steal the diamond. He turned out to be nothing short of a madman. His brother could be worse.

I hurried to the basement. The weapons bag Kane and Smoke got off the kid were moved there as a precaution since we were staying in his parent's home. If I was going to help stop Jordan. I would need some major firepower. I put my hand on the doorknob and suddenly felt faint. The dizziness from earlier had returned. I stopped moving after opening the door. My legs were getting weak as Abel flashed in my mind. The image of that monster terrified me. I turned around, scared of the man in front of me. Another flash of Abel appeared, and it caused me to scream. It wasn't like before when I was in the kitchen. Abel appeared all around me, and I backed away. I unexpectedly lost my footing and tumbled down the basement steps.

"Ah..." I cried as I came to a stop at the bottom step. I laid there crying, frightened at what I saw. My body began to ache all over. No woman should have to experience what I went through with that monster. I was letting Abel win. I felt defeated as a person...as a woman who just wanted to enjoy life. I thought the flashes would continue, but it stopped. It took all the strength in my arms to sit up straight against the wall. I couldn't help Kane if I couldn't help myself. And...he needs me. I had to be there for him.

I panted, trying to control my breathing became hard. *Calm down and get yourself together,* I thought. I saw what I had initially come to the basement for. Kane had moved a table against the back wall. It was covered by a cloth that draped down to the floor, hiding what was under it. I wiped the tears from my eyes. "Fuck Abel," I muttered. This was him trying to stop me...trying to prevent me from being there for Kane. I found the courage to stand on my feet, blocking out the pain as I stood. I closed my eyes and began to inhale and exhale slowly. I got my breathing under control before I began to move.

Each step I took towards the table reminded me of the fall. Women are recognized as being weak in difficult situations that men power through. That wouldn't be true today or any day.

282

There are women who are stronger than men, and I was one of them. I would show The Planner and Abel what we stand for. I made it to the table and lifted the cloth. I dragged the weapon's bag from under it. The load was heavier than I thought. I unzipped it and saw several guns that could cause damage. They would work, but that wasn't enough for me. I unloaded the guns, looking at each one as I placed them to the side. "There we go," I said, finding what I thought would get the job done. I saw a tag attached to the trigger handle and pulled it off. It read Bur 62mm. I guessed the seller labeled the weapon to identify the model. I knew it was a grenade launcher of some kind. It was smaller than any launcher I'd ever seen. I grabbed the weapon and put it on my shoulder, practicing how to hold it.

I finished looking through the bag and found only one rocket. It would have to do. Before I went back upstairs, I grabbed a small machine gun. It was an Uzi. I knew what the weapon could do from watching gangster movies. I left the other weapons on the floor and went upstairs. I didn't know how to use the Bur, so I went to Jar's officer and searched for how to use one on the computer. I found a video of a Russian man explaining it. I did exactly what he said and got the launcher loaded. The only thing I need to do was pull the trigger. I smiled as I left the house, grabbing the keys to Mrs. Simmon's Aston Martin. I put the weapons in the back seat and got in the car. It roared to life as I turned the key. "Here I come, baby," I said and sped from the driveway.

Chapter 54: Kane

I shielded my mother by covering over her on the ground. At first thought, it was The Planner who set this up. But that changed when I looked in their direction. Adrian, Jordan, and Rick all scrambled around looking for cover. The rocket was aimed at them, not us. I didn't see who exploded the plane, but Adrian did. He began to shoot at the attacker. I followed in the direction he had returned fire. "Kim!" I estimated her to be about thirty yards from us. She was standing next to my mother's Aston Martin with a rocket launcher.

I got up as she tossed the launcher on the ground. "Don't move," I told my mother. I turned to Bear and yelled. "Smoke is behind the plane!" I pointed in the direction. "Help him into the truck!" Bear hurried over to the giant plane. Bruce was already in position by the Humvee. I watched him get inside the driver seat and pull off toward Smoke.

I heard an extreme amount of gunfire erupt and ducked my head, reacting to the sound. I had to protect my mother and Kim. I fired at Adrian, trying to stop him from killing someone I love. I turned to Kim and saw her letting off with an assault weapon. I couldn't tell what it was, but it sounded like an Uzi. *Damn, she ain't playin',* I thought. She was here to protect me.

Rick fell to the ground with Jordan. I watched him struggle to get Jordan into the plane. I looked down at my mother. "No!" I

285

yelled. She wasn't by my side. That got me concerned when I didn't see her. The assault fire stopped. Kim had run out of ammunition. I searched around worriedly for my mother and spotted her next to Adrian. He pushed her inside the plane and fired at Kim. "Mother!" She turned around and stared at me. "Don't," I said in a low tone, praying she wouldn't leave me. It didn't work as I watched her vanish inside.

Kim had popped in another clip and began lightin' up the place. Adrian got inside the plane after running out of ammo. It would take him a few seconds to start the aircraft, giving me a choice to make. I could go after them or stop Kim from destroying the plane with my mother inside. "Kim!" I yelled, but she couldn't hear me over the gunfire. "Kim," I roared at the top of my lungs. She continued firing at the plane. She didn't notice my mother or Rick get inside the vehicle. "Fuck," I had to stop her before it was too late.

I watched the plane door shut. I ran as fast as I could over to Kim and screamed. "Stop!" as I waved my hands in the air for her to ceasefire. "Kim!"

She stopped the assault as I approached. "Kane," she said. "you ok, baby?"

"I'm fine," I said. "My mother and Rick are inside the plane."

"What," she said worriedly, "I didn't know."

Big Bruce skidded the Humvee to a stop next to us. Bear poked his head out of the window. "We have to get the fuck outta here. The feds are here." He pointed to several vehicles piling inside the impound, speeding our way.

"Shit," I picked up the rocket launcher and got in the driver seat. Kim hurried around to the passenger side. I saw the plane driving at high speed down the runway. There was nothing I could do to save my mother.

"Follow us," Bruce said and gunned the truck.

I floored the gas pedal, burning out the tires behind them. Two police vehicles drove in and blocked the entrance. The officers were still inside, and Bruce wasn't going to stop. I had to do something before he smashed the Humvee into the vehicles and possibly, kill the officers. I turned to Kim. "Learn out the window and shoot at the cops."

"What," she looked at me crazy.

"Miss them on purpose," I said. "I want to clear out the entrance."

"Ok," she leaned out of the window with the Uzi and fired at the police.

Big Bruce was seconds away from colliding with the cars, and several other vehicles sped past us. I checked the rearview. They were heading down the runway after the plane. I focused ahead and saw the two cop cars backing away, parting a clearance for us to escape. The truck nipped one of the police cruisers' side, and it spent out of control to a stop. The impact wasn't enough to harm the officer. They would be fine. I sped through the entrance onto the main road. I heard the tires squeal as I made a hard right turn. We made our getaway, and so did Jordan as the plane soared over the car. My heart stopped as I watched my mother fly away with two dangerous men.

Chapter 55: Kane

I thought about my mother on the way back to the house. Everything lined up in our favor to get her back safely. Why did she choose to remain with Jordan? I couldn't get what she said to me off my mind.

You wouldn't understand...I have to go with them. Take care of yourself.

She said it as if I would never see her again and not because she was in danger. It felt like something more. I stayed quiet for most of the trip home. Kim gently placed her hand over mine. I looked at her and slightly smiled even though it was difficult. She didn't say a word. The concerned expression on her face was more than enough. She could see through my smile that not bringing my mother home destroyed me.

I checked the rearview mirror before turning onto my block. There weren't any police vehicles in sight, just Bruce tailing us in the Humvee. We were safe from the law. I pulled the car in the driveway and shut off the motor. I put my head back and sighed.

Kim held my hand tightly. "I'm sorry," she said sincerely. "I could've killed her."

"I'm not worried about that," I told her. "it wasn't your fault." I straightened up and looked at her.

"But-"

"No ands, ifs, or buts about it," I smiled. "you were awesome. Adrian could've killed me. You saved me and everyone else."

She looked down shyly at our hands as she fiddled with my fingers. "I love you."

I lifted her head by the chin. "I love you more," and softly kissed her on the lips.

"No, you don't," she looked in the eyes.

"I'll let that slid," I said. "only because you came through with a rocket launcher."

"Don't forget about the Uzi," she joked.

"A'ight," I smiled. "gangsta."

"And don't you forget it," she kissed my lips a second time.

I heard a bang on my side window. It was Bruce. Bear was standing at the door, holding Smoke up by the arm. "Shit, I need you to take care of Smoke." I opened the door and got out.

"What happened?" She shut the car door and met me in the front.

"He got shot in the leg," I got to the front door and unlocked it.

"Fuck," Smoke said as Bear helped him inside. "I'ma body that bitch ass nigga."

Bear settled Smoke on the couch. Kim went to get the first aid kit. I walked up to Big Bruce and said, "shit got real back there," I held out my hand. "thanks for not bailing on us."

Bruce looked down at my hands. "I couldn't let anything happen to you," he smiled and shook my hand. "I still owe you an ass whoopin'."

I smiled back, "no doubt."

Kim came back with the med-kit. "Put your leg up on the couch," she told Smoke.

Smoke did what she asked, and she went to work.

"Kane," Bear gave me a serious look. "I have to tell you something, and you won't like what I have to say."

"What is it," I asked worriedly.

"You might want to sit down for this," Bear had a concerned look in his eyes.

"Brah," I said. "I've already been through it. Just tell me."

"A'ight," Bear took a deep breath and slowly exhaled. "Rick said Jordan and that guy Adrian work for your mother."

"Get the fuck outta here," I erupted sarcastically. "that's some bullshit."

"I'm just telling you what he said," Bear shrugged. "he mentioned the headquarters in Africa. The money, guns...he knew about everything."

"I can't believe it," I said. "you must've heard wrong. Jordan kidnapped my mother and convinced her to take him to the headquarters. He threatened her in some kind of way. She would've told me when we spoke."

"Did he?" Bear looked at me with raised eyebrows.

"You mean to tell me you believe that shit?" I was heated but not with Bear. The fact Rick would tell him that pissed me off. I was beyond mad...I was on fire.

"Your mother held me at gunpoint," Bruce spoke up. "I don't know about Rick or anything Bear is speaking of, but what I do know is she saved that guy from me. I was about to kill him. She told me to help him inside the truck after I beat him down. She gave the orders, and he listened. I thought that shit was odd or because she had the gun. But to me...it felt like they were in cahoots. She could've popped him right then and there. Shit would've been over. Instead, she made me drive to the impound."

"Kane," Kim said, and I looked at her. "I know it's hard for you, but you told me your father made over seven hundred million. Don't you think that's enough money to work with someone you don't see as a friend? Your mother can't tell the feds about it. She's probably using them to get the money. That's the only explanation I see of why she would get on the plane with them."

"From what I heard," Smoke spoke up. "mom wants the money but is also trying to protect you." He groaned as Kim continued to work on his leg. "We waited around for a month for The Planner to bust a move on us. This would explain why we didn't hear from him. They were after a plane, fam. I knew you don't wanna hear this, but mom offered him some bread."

I didn't respond to any of them. Thinking about what Rick said to Bear was mind-boggling. I sat down on the sofa, shocked at what could be true. Jordan, Adrian, and my mother...working together. I ran what she told me in my mind, trying to piece it all together.

You wouldn't understand...I have to go with them. Take care of yourself.

Of course, I wouldn't understand that you choose to work with a madman. Maybe you want to protect me, or it could be you want to keep what my father slaved for, or maybe...you just want the money, and you're using The Planner to get it. Whatever it is, mother, I won't let you do it alone, I thought. I stood up after coming to a conclusion.

Every eye in the room was on me, anticipating what I was about to say.

"Ah shit," Smoke smiled with a sense of knowing my next move. "We're goin' to Africa."

293

Author Bio

King Coopa J was born December 24, 1983, in Indianapolis, Indiana. He began writing fiction while incarcerated in 2010. Reading street literature inspired him to become a writer. He also has a passion for reading mystery, thriller & suspense novels. Kane, his first book, was created after making a bet with an inmate that he could write a novel. He currently lives in Maryland with his two sons.

Check out all of my books on Amazon!

Made in the USA
Coppell, TX
09 May 2021